DR. COSMOS

SHAURYA SAHAY

BLUEROSE PUBLISHERS
India | U.K.

Copyright © Shaurya Sahay 2024

All rights reserved by author. No part of this publication may be reproduced, stored in a retrieval system or transmitted in any form or by any means, electronic, mechanical, photocopying, recording or otherwise, without the prior permission of the author. Although every precaution has been taken to verify the accuracy of the information contained herein, the publisher assume no responsibility for any errors or omissions. No liability is assumed for damages that may result from the use of information contained within.

BlueRose Publishers takes no responsibility for any damages, losses, or liabilities that may arise from the use or misuse of the information, products, or services provided in this publication.

For permissions requests or inquiries regarding this publication, please contact:

BLUEROSE PUBLISHERS
www.BlueRoseONE.com
info@bluerosepublishers.com
+91 8882 898 898
+4407342408967

ISBN: 978-93-5819-709-9

Cover design: Suruchi
Typesetting: Tanya Raj Upadhyay

First Edition: January 2024

Preface

When I first started writing this book, I thought it would be a piece of cake. It turned out to be a layered cake where each layer is a variation of self-doubt, rejection and plot holes.

Most of my writing sessions went without a single word being written. I realized writing is the only activity where you can stare at a blank screen for hours and call it "working".

But after eight months of writing, I finally finished my first draft. However, I didn't like it at all. So, another five or six months passed, and I had written a completely new book, whose edited version is in your hands.

If I had to summarize the writing process in one word I would say 'Sandwich'. And, no, it's not because I'm hungry.

The first draft is like bread, dry, boring, and bland. The editing process is the filling. It's messy, but it's fun. And, voila! What you have in front of you is something an avid reader or glutton will finish in one sitting.

Most of the characters in this book are a figment of imagination, save for some that are drawn from mythology. I have written such characters from the stories, and myths I have heard. If I have gotten any facts or characteristics of such mythological characters wrong, please understand that it is in the best of intentions towards creativity and that not meant to hurt anybody's sentiments.

I used ChatGPT to write certain scenes in this book, such as when Shawn performs a medical surgery as I did not know about the procedure followed to perform a neurosurgery. The first chapter in this book was edited by ChatGPT to fix my rather informal and casual tone.

Finding a publisher for this book was a tough job. We reached out to many publishers. Then, just like Shawn stumbled upon Creator and her team, we happened to connect with Blue Rose. Thankfully, our encounter had a much better result. After a prolonged discussion, here we are, together with Blue Rose, happy to present before you the book: Dr Cosmos.

I would like to thank Suruchi, the illustrator of this book, for creating such a wonderful piece of art. I would also like to thank every single person on the team handling this project.

I hope you enjoy reading the story of Shawn Stephalla, as he embarks on a journey across the galaxy in an attempt to redeem himself from his own self-prejudice. Nobody will fight your battles for you, especially the one that exist in your mind.

If this preface has managed to pique your interest, I would not like to take any more of your time on this appetizer, as the main course lies ahead. Happy reading!

Table of Contents

Chapter 1 Shawn Stephalla 1
Chapter 2 Miss Void Returns 7
Chapter 3 Galactic Regicide 10
Chapter 4 A Peculiar Encounter 13
Chapter 5 The Fateful Tumour 22
Chapter 6 Oops 25
Chapter 7 The Tale of Miss Void 30
Chapter 8 Cosmos messes up 35
Chapter 9 Creator's Truth 43
Chapter 10 Creator loses her Powers 48
Chapter 11 Escape 51
Chapter 12 The Crucial Decision 55
Chapter 13 Hyperspeed 60
Chapter 14 Brim Typhoonian 64
Chapter 15 A New Hero 67
Chapter 16 An Epic Dogfight 76
Chapter 17 Miss Void Appears. Again. Hooray 82
Chapter 18 Miss Void's Prisoner 85
Chapter 19 The God of the Sky Comes to Help 89
Chapter 20 The Worst Kind of Prison 95

Chapter 21 The Neptunian and The Tyrant 103

Chapter 22 Duel of the Celestials 107

Chapter 23 Creator's Sacrifice 111

Chapter 24 The King of the Galaxy 115

Chapter 25 It was all Just a Dream. Or was it... ? 118

Epilogue 1 120

Epilogue 2 125

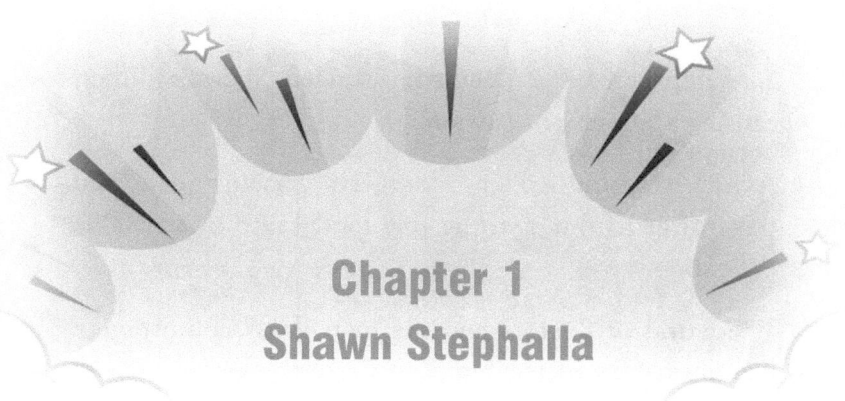

Chapter 1
Shawn Stephalla

Shawn found himself in the cold, sterile hush of the hospital waiting room, his eyes locked onto a closed door.

Yet, he wasn't really staring at the door; his thoughts had spun into a web of their own.

The strong smell of cleaning detergent engulfed the room. However, that was the one thing he despised at the moment.

Behind that door, his father lay on an operating table, a patient instead of the skilled surgeon he'd always wanted to be.

The event that had led to this grim moment was just a slip on a freshly mopped floor, a small misstep with colossal repercussions.

It was Mr. Wenderson, a friend of Shawn's dad, who recounted the accident.

The impact of the fall had wounded Shawn's father, causing a serious concussion.

As he was rushed into surgery, Shawn's dad had transformed from a strong role model into a vulnerable patient.

The world of doctors and the marvels of neurosurgery had always fascinated him, but those things never quite captured Shawn's imagination the way they had his father's.

The door creaked open, and Shawn's focus snapped to it like a moth to a flame. A surgeon emerged, a familiar face due to his father's connections.

The doctor's expression seemed oddly composed, almost strained, as he approached Shawn with careful tugs at his coat sleeves.

Shawn's voice trembled with apprehension, "What happened? Is he okay"

Tears glistened in the surgeon's eyes, casting a shadow over Shawn's heart. The unease he'd felt turned to dread.

"I... I'm really sorry, Shawn," Mr. Wenderson's voice faltered, heavy with tragedy.

Shawn's breath caught, his chest constricting. This couldn't be real. "No, he just slipped. It's not possible— "

"Shawn, your father... he's gone."

A surge of denial crashed over Shawn, disbelief warring with reality. "No, he can't be gone. He can't leave me."

Caught between disbelief and heartache, Shawn's gaze bore into Mr. Wenderson's eyes. Accusation hung heavy in the air, the weight of the situation almost too much to bear. "You're a neurosurgeon," his voice quivered, anger and sorrow intertwined. "His head was hurt. Why couldn't you save him?"

"Shawn, that wasn't within my scope," Mr. Wenderson's voice softened, offering a hint of understanding. "The injury caused severe bleeding from the back of his head."

Each word was a hammer blow to Shawn's fragile reality. The truth he fought against was settling in, bit by bit. His wails of anguish filled the air as grief threatened to overwhelm him.

This poignant moment of loss mingled with the memory of another heartbreak.

The echoes of his school day intertwined with the hospital lobby silence.

Shawn's day had started so differently, his thoughts consumed by his upcoming birthday party during a math lesson.

"Stephalla," the teacher's voice broke through his reverie. "STEPHALLA!"

Startled, Shawn snapped back, stumbling over his words. "Y-Yes, sir."

"Want to answer the question?"

His gaze shifted to the board, where no question was written. Quick with math but slow to pay attention, he realized there was no question there.

"Sir, you haven't written the question."

Laughter erupted from the class, their amusement at his expense an old tune he knew all too well.

"Weren't you paying attention?"

Embarrassment flushed his cheeks, but his mind wasn't on his teacher's reprimand. It was consumed by his own thoughts, a shield against potential humiliation.

He muttered an apology that felt like 'sorry, sir.'

"And you should be. Just because you're a teacher's ward doesn't mean you're exempt from rules."

"No, sir."

"Sit down."

As he settled into his seat, a knock interrupted the class. Anxiety coiled in his chest as the principal walked in— a harbinger of bad news. This couldn't be good, especially with Mr. Nanton already in a foul mood.

"I need to talk to Mr. Stephalla."

His heart skipped a beat, foreboding filling him. His apprehension, though, was nothing compared to the blow he was about to receive.

The principal's words hit Shawn like a tidal wave.

His father, the biology teacher, had met with an accident. A wet floor and a water fountain's iron rod had combined forces to bring his father to this dire state. Severe bleeding from the back of his head, they said.

In that instant, Shawn's world crumbled. The school's familiar walls and his classmates' laughter blurred as grief consumed him. The weight of loss pressed upon him, merging with the pain of the present.

Unbeknownst to him, this new layer of agony would amplify the echoes of an earlier heartbreak and shape his future in ways he couldn't yet fathom.

***

His mother guided him home, a beacon of solace amidst the storm of sadness.

Seeking refuge in his room, Shawn's eyes fell on a neatly wrapped box and a folded letter on his bed. He reached for the letter first, his father's handwriting a poignant reminder of the man who was no more.

Shawn,

I intended to give you this letter on your tenth birthday, but I'm afraid I have to come home late as I will be leaving for a field trip.

Allow me to share a story: In my youth, I aspired to be a doctor, yearning to heal and save lives. Yet, life's path led me elsewhere. I just want you to know that my deepest wish for you is to be a beacon of help and compassion, whatever path you choose.

Shawn's tears fell, staining the paper as he absorbed the words.

A sense of purpose took root within him, sparked by his father's unwavering ideals. With determination, he folded the letter and placed it beside him.

From that moment onward, Shawn Stephalla pledged to himself that he would become a beacon of hope, honoring his father's legacy by bringing light to the lives of others.

Little did he know what a complicated web fate could weave.

Away from planet Earth, a woman barged into the Galactic Palace that resided in the center of the sun.

A woman who, would one day clash paths with Shawn.

Chapter 2
Miss Void Returns

The royal court of the Milky Way Galaxy was eagerly waiting for the chief informer of the court.

"How much more time will we have to wait?" asked the Minister of the court, impatiently tapping his feet. The Minister was dressed in a sleek black pinstriped suit that he had acquired from Earth.

"It shouldn't take more than a few minutes for him to reach," said the king. The king sat in the center of the throne room, his white battle suit in stark contrast with his dark and tall figure.

"But what news could be so important that we have to wait for him for five hours?" asked the Deputy Minister, his slick moustache shimmering in the dim light of the room.

"I don't know." said the king, glancing at his spear.

After a few more minutes, there was a knock on the door. The informer had arrived

"What urgent news do you bring for us?" asked the king, sitting upright on his throne.

"I bring bad news my king," said the informer. His clothes were torn and his face was blackened with soot. As if there had been an explosion in front of him.

"What news could be so distressing?" said the king.

"Your majesty, there has been an escape from the Galactic Jail!" The informer dropped to his knees, and panted.

The king was obviously distressed at this news.

"But that is the most secure jail in the whole of the Milky Way, how could someone escape from it?" asked the king.

"My lord it is... it is Miss Void!" Whispered the informer.

This news apparently didn't shock the king.

"Who the heck is Miss Void?" asked the king.

The Minister's face darkened. He turned to the king, a distressed expression on his face.

"If Miss Void has escaped, then this is very bad news indeed."

"But why-

Suddenly, as if on cue, the royal court's door turned to dust!

The dust cleared, to reveal a woman that stood at the threshold. She wore a green suit with dark red highlights and a psychotic smile. In her right hand, she held a sword with the illusion of dust on the tip.

She laughed a hollow, deep chuckle.

It was Miss Void.

Chapter 3
Galactic Regicide

The moment he saw her, the king reached for his sword but Miss Void was too fast for him. She swiftly glided across the floor and kicked the king's sword out of his hands.

"Where is Creator?" She asked. She longed to finally exact revenge on that wretched liar.

"Wh-Who?" stammered the king.

"So you don't know Creator. I wish I could be that oblivious. How can you be king if you don't even know the second-most powerful being in the galaxy?" The woman studied the king, probably trying to judge his intellect.

"S-Second best?"

"Well naturally," she advanced, fiddling with the handle of her sword, "I'm first. But still-

She turned to the bunch of (useless) ministers, who were seated on their thrones, gawping.

"Surely one of you airheads knows Creator?" She asked. After there was no response, she plunged her face into her palms.

"you all-are-USELESS!" She bellowed. "Why have you been admitted into this reputed council if you don't know a thing about your own GALAXY! Fine, I will rule this galaxy by myself, and my first decree will be to fire ALL OF YOU!"

"I won't let that happen!" The king seemed to have found courage somewhere in that pitiable body of his and held his spear in his hands again, aiming it at Miss Void.

"Step aside, insolent fool!" She shouted. "I do not waste my time fighting losers."

The king let out a guttural cry and swung his spear, only to have it blocked by Miss Void.

The ministers watched as the king and Miss Void dueled, sword against spear.

After sparks of energy flew from their magical weapons, the king managed to cut Miss Void's eyebrow with his spear.

Miss Void looked away, and the king whacked her with the blunt of his spear.

"Aaaaaarghhhh!"

The king leaped into the air, aiming to hurtle his spear at Miss Void, but she lodged her sword into the king's chest.

The spear dropped out of the king's hands. Miss Void yanked out her sword, rolled over and stood up.

The king fell to the floor.

Then his arms turned to dust. Then his legs, then his body, and then his face.

"Wh-What happened?" Asked a Minister

Miss Void turned, straightening her hair out of her face.

"I have killed your beloved king." She said coldly. "I am now your queen and you will bow to me."

Not wanting to turn into dust, the ministers got up and bowed, trembling with fear.

Chapter 4
A Peculiar Encounter

Fifteen years later, Shawn Stephalla had pursued his dream of becoming a neurosurgeon. His days were filled with saving lives, one delicate operation at a time. Today was no different as he completed a successful surgery on a patient with a brain tumor. With a quick moment of respite, Shawn received a call from the nurse's station.

Another patient awaited his expertise in the operating theater.

Rushing through the bustling hospital corridors, Shawn reached the operating theater with a determined stride.

The nurses, familiar faces he had come to know and trust, greeted him with warm smiles.

Their interactions were a blend of professional camaraderie and lighthearted banter, which helped alleviate the tension that hung in the air.

As Shawn entered the sterile environment of the operating room, he noticed the patient lying on the surgical table, surrounded by the latest medical equipment.

The monitors hummed with vital signs, displaying a complex web of data, and the anesthesia team stood ready by the patient's side.

With a calm demeanor, Shawn began scrubbing his hands meticulously, following the strict protocols of sterile preparation. As he donned his surgical gown and gloves, his focus shifted entirely to the task at hand— the delicate and intricate operation that lay ahead.

Shawn started by carefully positioning the patient's head and securing it with specialized headrests. He ensured that the patient's body was properly supported, maintaining a comfortable position throughout the surgery.

Using a surgical marker, Shawn marked the incision site on the patient's scalp, following the preoperative imaging and surgical plan.

He discussed the procedure with the assisting surgical team, confirming the specifics of the tumor's location and the surgical approach.

An anesthesiologist closely monitored the patient's vital signs, administering the appropriate medications to induce general anesthesia and ensure the patient's comfort and safety throughout the procedure.

Shawn prepared the surgical site by sterilizing the scalp and applying sterile drapes to maintain a sterile field. With a scalpel, he made a precise incision through the scalp, carefully considering the optimal length and placement to provide sufficient access to the tumor.

Using specialized surgical instruments, Shawn skillfully dissected through the layers of tissue, working his way down to the skull.

He used an electric drill and a specialized bone saw to create a small opening in the skull, called a burr hole, through which he gained access to the brain.

With the help of a surgical microscope, Shawn carefully visualized the brain and identified the tumor's borders.

He employed microsurgical techniques to navigate around critical structures, such as blood vessels and healthy brain tissue, while gradually removing the tumor.

Shawn used a combination of suction devices, microscissors, and delicate forceps to remove the tumor piece by piece.

Throughout the process, he periodically used intraoperative imaging, such as MRI or CT scans, to ensure precise tumor resection while minimizing damage to healthy brain tissue.

Once the tumor was completely removed, Shawn meticulously inspected the surgical site, ensuring no remnants remained. He then took steps to control any bleeding, using electrocautery or specialized clips as needed.

With the tumor excised and the surgical site clear, Shawn meticulously closed the layers of tissue and the skull using absorbable sutures and surgical staples, ensuring a secure and watertight closure.

After the operation, Shawn ordered postoperative imaging to confirm the extent of tumor resection and evaluate the patient's condition.

The anesthesia team expertly managed the patient's transition out of anesthesia while closely monitoring vital signs.

Another successful operation completed.

In the night, right next to Shawn's house, a blue beam of light struck the ground.

The beam retracted back into the sky, leaving four strange beings behind.

"This is the spot you chose?" Said a man who, despite the cold, was wearing only a gold chest-plate. His stomach, and well chiseled abs were revealed, yet he didn't shiver.

Some passers-by were staring at the gold crown on his head. He waved his hand at them and muttered something at them in Sanskrit. They turned around and started walking in the opposite direction.

"Mortals," he said. "See something out of the ordinary and they stare at it like it's a dead dragon's liver,"

"That was oddly specific, Indra," said another being. His skin was deep blue and he wore a gold and green armor on his torso.

Paired with it was another royal and manly piece of clothing: beach shorts.

"Yes, well, I can only say I've seen it from my own two eyes."

"Don't you mean with?" Asked another being. He wore a pinstriped suit and black jeans. But his boots were made of silver.

"Yes whatever," was the lightning god's lazy reply.

"Boys, you can squabble later, we've got work to do." Said a woman with multi-colored hair and a gold armor chest plate strapped to an orange polo T-shirt.

She walked up to the house and opened it with the keys.

Once they were inside, they all settled sown and Indra somehow produced snacks and beverages.

"Indra, we're having a serious discussion about the fate of the galaxy, not a tea party!" Exclaimed Snogglebrout, the blue-skinned Neptunian.

"Hey," Minister, the pinstriped chief reached out for a fruit cake. "smackhs shelp ahvereyshink." he managed to say while stuffing the entire dessert into his mouth.

He meant to say 'Snacks help anything' but with that much food in his mouth, it was a marvel if he could even grunt.

Indra reached out for a glass of soma but all the edibles vanished with a wispy trail of blue.

"Let's focus shall we?" Said Creator, the woman with multi-colored hair. "What should we do?"

"Isn't that obvious," asked Indra, "We just make another Celestial."

"It isn't that easy. The ritual can only be conducted upon a human of pure heart. If he isn't of pure heart... well, we don't want another Miss Void. So we first have to start scouting for a worthy human."

"Why don't we start with blonde-head over here," Snogglebrout jabbed his thumb to the left. "Your neighbor next door seems like a pretty good option."

"Well he needs to be willing."

"Very well then, go on and ask him." Said Indra.

"Are you mad? I can't just walk up to him."

"Then what?"

"We'll have to contact him somehow, and you know, get to know him. Then after a few days we can tell him."

"Why do you have to wait this long?" Asked Indra "If I wanted I could just strike anybody with a lightning bolt filled with powers and send Shrui and Uchchaishravas to get them."

"Well we can't," said Snogglebrout, "Creator can you tell us how far Miss Void has progressed in tracking you down."

"Fortunately, not very much," Creator turned to an oddly placed curtain. She waved her hand.

The curtain fell down revealing a board with snippets of articles from the Daily Star (the newspaper distributed throughout the galaxy).

They were all connected with wispy blue strands of light.

"Creator?" Said Indra, "I can totally understand all of this, but can you tell me the important thing-just for confirmation, I mean, I can understand this-but tell me if she suspects Earth as your base."

Minister smirked. "Ask me. I'm her most trusted minister, and I can confirm that she most definitely doesn't. So you, your minions and Amravati are safe for the time being."

"Phew. Thank the Heavens!"

***

Shawn parked in his garage after a long, tiring day of work.

After taking a nice hot bath and eating his dinner (a cold, dry Spicy McChicken and a bag of peri-peri fries from McDonald's drive- through.)

I know right, not very healthy.

And he's supposed to be a doctor. But, it had been a tiring day, and Shawn really didn't want to cook.

Anyways, after wolfing down his dinner he went to bed, and was setting his alarm when he saw a blue, wispy light glow in the house next to him.

Now, this would seem kind of normal, if someone just had a really strong lamp, but no one had moved into this house for nine months.

He saw four silhouettes from the window, and none of them looked normal.

As you would expect, he walked out in his orange pajamas, a fashion statement to rival Elton John, and set out to investigate.

He rang the doorbell.

"No, Indra I'll get it," he heard a voice inside say.

Hmm. 'Indra' sounds like a weird name..

Then he realized Indra was the Hindu god of the sky. He rode a white elephant and had a seven headed horse named something confusing. Strange.

A woman answered the door, and it may have been rude but Shawn's first question was,

"What happened to your hair?"

She smiled, looking at her multi-colored hair. "Oh, just keeping up with the trends. So, are you the doctor that lives next door?"

"I'm a surgeon, yes. I just came to see if everything's alright, I saw a bluish sort of light from your window."

"Oh, your mind's playing tricks on you honey. You should go and get a good night's sleep."

"Okay then, bye. Nice meeting you."

The door closed with a bang.

Shawn stood there in the cold, at night in the middle of the street in his pajamas for a few seconds and he could have sworn he'd heard more than one voice say 'Phew!'.

Chapter 5
The Fateful Tumor

Overall, it had been a challenging day for Shawn.

He had woken up late and rushed to work. Little did he know that the afternoon held an even greater trial in store for him. He received an urgent call to perform a surgery— a delicate brain tumor resection. While Shawn initially approached it with confidence, unaware of the impending turn of events, he soon realized that fate had a different plan.

As he entered the operating theater, his mind was preoccupied with thoughts of the upcoming action movie he had planned to watch with his friend.

The patient, Mrs. Wilson, lay on the surgical table, ready for the procedure.

Shawn engaged with his team, cracking a few lighthearted jokes to ease the tension and create a supportive atmosphere.

With a focused mindset, Shawn began the surgery, skillfully making the necessary incisions and working his way toward the brain tumor. The atmosphere in the room was a mix of concentration and muted conversation, highlighting the collaborative effort of the surgical team.

But then, an unexpected complication arose. Mrs. Wilson experienced a sudden cardiac arrest.

Panic gripped the room as alarms blared, and the team sprang into action. Shawn's heart raced as he took charge of the situation, orchestrating the resuscitation efforts.

"Code Blue! Cardiac arrest!" shouted Daniel, his voice filled with urgency.

Shawn's training and experience kicked in as he directed the team in performing cardiopulmonary resuscitation (CPR), providing chest compressions, and administering medications to revive Mrs. Wilson's failing heart.

The room buzzed with a flurry of activity as everyone worked tirelessly to save her life.

Despite their efforts, the situation grew dire. The beeping of the heart monitor gradually slowed until it eventually fell silent.

Shawn's hands trembled, and a wave of profound sadness washed over him.

The room fell into an eerie silence, broken only by the sound of his heavy, labored breaths.

Daniel, his voice filled with sorrow, turned to Shawn and softly asked, "What happened?"

The moment took Shawn back fifteen years, when his father died. For a moment, the elderly patient's face was replaced with his father's.

In that moment, Shawn's emotions overwhelmed him. "We... We couldn't save her," he whispered, his voice laden with regret.

The weight of the patient's loss, coupled with the reminder of his father's fate, felt unbearable.

The team stood in stunned silence, their expressions reflecting a shared sense of grief.

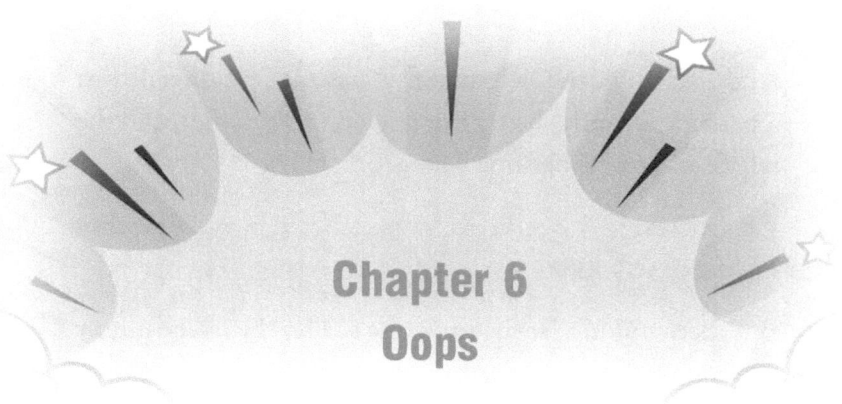

Chapter 6
Oops

To say that Shawn took it lightly would have been a grave mistake.

He took a leave of four days which he spent living entirely in his head.

Now, having someone pass away while you're operating is not uncommon. Most people are sad for a few days, then they wave it off. Because, really, it's not exactly your fault. The patient started getting hyper and went into cardiac arrest which you were totally unprepared for, so what can you do about it?

But that's not how Shawn took it.

To him, it wasn't just a patient that he lost. It was confidence.

Confidence, that he was a great, accomplished surgeon.

And also, it doesn't help that this was the first time he lost a patient. And that he was reminded of his father, and the whole reason he became a surgeon.

He became a surgeon to save other's lives while not having to risk his.

But he couldn't save someone's life. He felt utterly useless.

But then, for the first time in three days something jerked him out of his long thought.

BOOM!!

The house next door exploded in a burst of blue light!

"Snogglebrout, what did you do!" Said Creator.

"Oops?" He said.

The four of them, Minister, Indra, Creator, and Snogglebrout were standing in the middle of the street.

Their house had exploded because Snogglebrout had accidentally slipped down the staircase and crashed into the cloud of transformative energy Creator had made to turn their recruit into a Celestial.

The explosion had caused the cloud to develop faster, but now they were exposed in the middle of the street with a huge cloud of light standing between them.

"Crap." Said Indra, "We'll have to use it on someone fast, or else this thing will explode, and the entire street will go boom."

"Yes, no need to point out that nerve racking fact." Snapped Minister.

Right then, the blonde guy next door came rushing out in... his pajamas, again?

Does that guy roam around in his pajamas all the time? Thought Creator.

"Whoa," He noticed the cloud of energy.

"What the-

His exclamation of surprise was cut short by a deafening crackling sound from the aggressive cloud.

Indra looked at her, then gestured mutely towards Stephalla. The noise increased and Creator knew that if someone didn't step into it in five seconds, the entire city will explode. The impact would be worse than a nuclear missile.

And Creator understood his message.

"Excuse me Shawn,"

He looked at her.

"What?" He asked blankly.

"I need a favor-

Two more seconds.

-I need you to step into this cloud-

One second. Creator used her mental powers to slow time for a bit. But it wouldn't last long.

"What! Are you crazy? You want me to step into-

Half a second was remaining, and Creator made a rash decision. She shoved Shawn towards the giant oval cloud.

Shawn fell into the cloud and the crackling stopped.

The cloud started wrapping itself around him with little tendrils of blue fog.

Soon, he was completely immersed in the blue fog. There was a sort of metal clanking which indicated armor being formed.

After a minute, the cloud completely faded away and a new being stood there, limping like a lifeless ragdoll.

It had green skin which, when leading to his face turned into normal human color. He had the same face, with dirty blonde hair, a slight stubble and glasses.

It wore beige armor with little blue lights, a purple triangle and a large red cape.

"What-Am-I?" It said.

A smirk appeared on Creator's face.

"You, my wonderful creation, are the silver lining for the whole galaxy. You are the hero, and the soon to be king of the Milky Way.

You are-COSMOS!"

Chapter 7
The Tale of Miss Void

Did you ever have a moment in your life, when something happens and you just didn't have a say in the matter. Well, if you did then I believe you'll relate a bit with Shawn Stephalla. Or, should I say Cosmos?

Imagine, from being a depressed, sulking and self-hating person, he became a super-powered, multi-colored, weird sort of meta-alien-humanoid.

He was told by the strange residents of that house that he had to defeat this evil, woman who had usurped power of the galaxy.

Quite a leap.

And of course Shawn wasn't prepared.

It took him at least two hours to explore his powers and, thank god, Minister had suggested that they go to an empty field so that no one finds a hole in their house when they reach.

"Whoa, this is so cool."

"Yeah, just you wait," snorted Indra, "We'll see how cool this is when you go up against Miss Void."

"So anyone going to train me or anything?"

For some reason, this caused Snogglebrout to erupt in laughter.

"... train? you?"

Creator silenced him with a hard stare.

"No one's gonna have to train you, you'll just learn on your own. The skills will come naturally to you when you have to fight."

"So, you mean I'll only learn when I have to fight for my life?"

"Yes."

He decided to drop that conversation.

When they were back in Shawn's home, Indra had welcomed himself into Shawn's kitchen, and came out grabbing every single bag of chips Shawn had. And he had apparently looked at Shawn's collection of soda bottles.

"You're a madman. That number of Cokes is unholy."

"It's my comfort food."

"Comfort food? Pfft. That product has been created by a giant, cola flavored belch."

Everyone decided not to expand on Indra's theory.

Cosmos turned to Creator.

"So, what was the name of that evil woman again?"

"I would rather not mention her, but its 'Miss Void'."

"So, how did she become evil and everything?"

He could see he had pressed a soft spot.

"But it's okay of you'd rather not-

"No. If you're going to stop her, I think you should know everything."

Asteroid B-79, Milky Way Galaxy, 1975

Creator stood in an asteroid's craters watching as Jennifer Smith stepped into the blue cloud of energy swirling in front of them.

With her stood the king of the galaxy, and his entire army.

The king had grown old, and he needed an heir to rule the galaxy. But as he did not have a child, he asked Creator, his old friend, to create a Celestial who could take over the throne.

The blue tendrils wrapped around Jennifer.

She had agreed to this only because of one reason: she felt useless.

She had been fired from her job and had gone broke within a month. Creator had found her and offered to make her powerful and promised her that she would rule the galaxy.

After the cloud faded, a Celestial stepped out.

She wore a green suit with horns coming out of a helmet, and she held a sword with the illusion of dust on the tip.

Oh no. That was a bad sign. If a Celestial was born alongside a weapon, they would most probably turn out evil.

But they decided to ignore that.

Creator couldn't think of a name for her, and Jennifer didn't have her memories so she was called 'Jen'.

But a few days later the king called Jennifer and told her that his wife was expecting a baby. So, with a heavy heart, he told Jen that she would not be able to rule anymore.

"I'll tell you what, I'll make you the Commander of my army, how's that sound?"

Miss Void was quiet. Then she spoke.

"You. You-are-a-LIAR!"

She latched out with her sword, and tried to attack the king.

A duel ensued, sword against spear.

But the king was more skilled a warrior than her, and disarmed her quickly. She tried to shoot green energy at him out of her palm, but he kicked her in the face and his hard metal boots caused her to pass out.

"Guards! Come and throw this woman into the Galactic Jail!"

When Jen regained consciousness she found herself locked in a cell. She tried blasting at the walls but the walls reflected the shots.

Jennifer started to grow even more evil in that cell, plotting her escape, and created a name for herself, a name that would go on to haunt millions. Miss Void.

... Creator paused and took a chip out of a Lays packet.

"When I heard the news that she'd escaped, I decided to create another Celestial, who would defeat her. I decided to make him the exact opposite of Miss Void, so I named him the opposite of a void. I named you after the cosmos, symbolizing your power, and that you will always protect the galaxy."

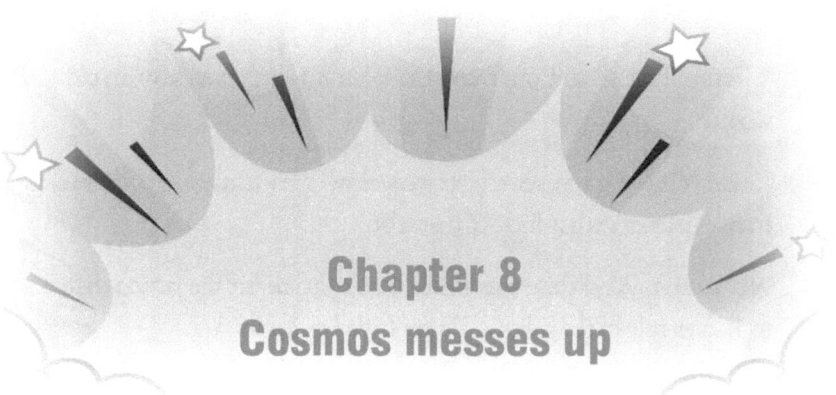

Chapter 8
Cosmos messes up

I bet most people would be pretty happy if they became one of the most powerful people in the Milky Way. Or at least they think they would.

Once you look away from the cool, flashy powers, you notice that it's actually a huge responsibility.

If there's a black hole about to devour a planet, or a race of evil aliens trying to invade you can't just dial up the police.

The people will look at you to help. You'll be expected to fight, to save the citizens of the galaxy.

And, suffering from recent low self-esteem, and self-distrust, Shawn didn't even glance at the flashy powers.

That may have been a problem because he unknowingly vaporized the grass in his back lawn, which they had moved into. So now they were back in the field and a battle was raging in Shawn's head.

Who am I kidding, I can't save the galaxy! I can't even save an old woman.

Dude! You've got super-cool powers now. You can erase someone from existence with a flick of the wrist!

No, I can't. And these four think that I can defeat the person that took over rule of the galaxy. I'll get killed in an instant.

No, you won't. You've got the same powers as her. Besides this is your chance to prove yourself again. If you couldn't save a patient, now you have the chance to save the entire galaxy.

Trillions of people out there, on different planets, are counting on you.

They don't even know I exist.

But their lives still depend on you!

"Uh oh," Said Minister.

"What?" Asked Cosmos, coming back from his battlefield of a mind.

"Your hands."

"What about them?"

But then he looked down and saw that a green sort of mist was flowing out his hands, and it had made a shape in the sky.

It was just a rectangle, with a triangle inside.

"Yes!" Exclaimed Creator.

"What?"

"That shape. It's the symbol of the cosmos, it shows that you're of pure heart."

"Wait a minute, the entire cosmos is symbolized in just a rectangle and a triangle?"

"Don't ask me, I wasn't there when it was chosen."

Just then, the sky rumbled.

"I think it may rain today," Said Cosmos.

But Indra looked concerned.

"Trust me when I say this," said the god of the sky, "That's not rain!"

And to confirm his statement a flying vehicle flew into eyesight

"It's a space-pod."

"What's a space-pod?"

"It's the vehicle the soldiers of the galactic army use to commute. Not a good sign."

A space pod flew down to the ground and large mechanical legs sprung from its metallic disc shaped body.

A door appeared out of nowhere, and a dozen weird humanoids came rushing out, all in army stance with rifle-like tools called Space-Ray blasters in their hands.

Another humanoid alien walked out of the pod. It seemed to be the boss. It looked the same as Snogglebrout except with different features, like one human looks different next to another but they're both still humans.

The boss started issuing out orders to his soldiers.

Snogglebrout made an angry grunting noise.

"Banbrine," he grumbled.

"Ah, old snog." Said Banbrine with the air of one meeting an old friend. But looking at Snogglebrout's expression, that was certainly not the case.

"That's not my name!"

"As if I care!"

Banbrine and Snogglebrout looked close to strangling each other, while Indra and Creator exchanged glances and Cosmos just stood there like an idiot.

Then Creator made a sudden movement, but Banbrine didn't notice.

Creator stretched out her hands and shot a blast of energy.

"Surprise, surprise-

But Banbrine's reflexes were really good.

He grabbed his spear, and absorbed her blast.

"You ain't getting the better of me, Creator,"

"Well I am," Snogglebrout grabbed his spear and caught Banbrine off guard.

Swoosh!

Banbrine clutched his eyebrow where a drop of blood trickled down his forehead.

"You little TRAITOR!" He roared.

Snogglebrout and Banbrine started to duel with their spears, and Creator and Indra fought off the soldiers. Minister, who had no powers stepped aside and threw the occasional punch to any soldier that came his way.

"Use your power." He grunted to Cosmos as his fist sailed wide of a soldiers face.

"Right." Said Cosmos, but by the time he lifted his hands, a soldier shot multiple lasers at him with his space-ray blaster.

He clutched the area where the laser had hit and fell in between Snogglebrout and Banbrine's fight.

Snogglebrout looked at him but by that time Banbrine leaped and plunged his spear into Snogglebrout's chest.

Snogglebrout gasped as Banbrine yanked the spear out. He fell to the ground and attracted everyone's attention.

There was dead silence. Literally.

Snogglebrout inhaled sharply. The battle paused, everyone looking in his direction.

"C-Creator," he gasped. "F-Finish the m-mission... "

He fell to the ground clutching his chest.

There was absolute silence.

Lord Indra looked at Banbrine with fury.

He flew into the air and emitted lightning from everywhere. Thunder roared in the sky.

Indra stretched his arms out to either side and caused so much lightning to strike the ground that the space-pods short-circuited after a bolt hit their engine.

Electricity crackled in Indra's eyes and his voice was amplified a hundred more times than its usual self.

"YOU'LL PAY FOR THAT, YOU STUCK UP PIECES OF CRAP!"

A hundred bolts of lightning struck the soldiers, and Indra sent a specifically dangerous one at Banbrine.

"And here's a word of advice," the King of God's voice suddenly seemed so low, that it was even more terrifying than his scream.

"Never. Ever. Mess. With a GOD!"

All the soldiers on the field got electrocuted by his ministorm. Except for Banbrine.

Indra landed on the ground.

Fear creeped up on Banbrine's face as he crawled backwards.

"You little scumbag." The Lord of the Sky grabbed Banbrine by his uniforms collar and flew into the sky. Lightning flashed in the sky. "You're dead meat."

Indra sent him crashing down the ground with a single punch.

Banbrine's limp body fell to the ground with a splat.

There was silence, mainly from the lack of alive beings.

But just then, as if they didn't have enough problems already, a woman materialized out of thin air.

She stood with her head bowed. A sword with the illusion of dust at the tip formed in her hand. She raised her head to get a good look at her victims.

Her evil smirk sent a chill down Cosmos' spine.

She practically glided towards them with her sword held in one hand and horns cutting through the air. She wore a dark green suit with red highlights and a red cape.

"Finally," she said. "After so many ages, I finally get to meet the cause of all my problems."

In a swift movement she knocked out Minister with a blast of purple energy. Creator raised her hand but found it to be cuffed by a lock of purple energy.

"Creator," said the woman.

"Miss Void," the former snarled.

"I suppose it would be to cliché to say 'we meet again!',"

"It would be too."

"Well, then how about we get past the formalities, and get on with the killing?"

Chapter 9
Creator's Truth

You won't be killing anyone." Cosmos said. Every inch of his soul was telling him to run away, but he had already lost one friend. Correction: he had caused him to die.

Shawn wasn't going to lose another. Not if he could help it. However, the way Miss Void looked at him, like she was just letting him live for the fun of it, told him he really didn't.

"Ha. Are you enjoying feeding false hopes to his one's mind too?" Said Miss Void, glancing at Creator.

"Creator what is she talking about?'

"Oh, you didn't tell him? You're even lower than I thought."

"Creator!"

"I don't know what she's talking about Cosmos,"

"Trust me darling, every word out of her mouth is a lie."

"Why should I listen to you?" He said. "You're the evil one here."

"But I'm afraid my dear," she gripped her sword more tightly. "That evil is in the eye of the beholder. It all matters on perspective."

She lunged, attempting to slice off Creator's neck, but Cosmos knocked her off with a shot of green energy.

"Why are you protecting her?" Miss Void asked, "Trust me, in the end, she's going to stab you in the back."

"Says the one holding a sword," rebuked Cosmos.

"I can see. She has blinded you with a sense of righteousness, I bet she told you that you will be the king of the galaxy after you kill me?"

Wait a minute, thought Shawn. That's true.

"She must've told you that the entire galaxy will look up to you. That you'll protect the entire Milky Way. It's true isn't it. ISN'T IT?"

"Yes, it is."

"Then believe me when I say that, all these promises will shatter the moment you ask for them."

"No." Shawn had thought he finally came on the right track. He couldn't let the one he was supposed to kill challenge his beliefs of right and wrong.

"You're trying to confuse me aren't you?"

Power lit up in his hand, and Indra tried to strike Miss Void, but she constantly shifted her position, making it impossible for Cosmos and Indra to even touch her. But she managed to speak.

"If you want to know everything then let me tell you the truth."

She spread her hands and looked up at the sky. She gave another one of her signature evil smirks.

Shawn gasped. For a moment he didn't even remember his own name, then it all came flooding back to him. He saw Miss Void standing in front of him.

He tried to extend his hands but he found they were chained. He lunged at her but his entire body was chained up by purple energy.

"Struggling will not help you in any way," said her cold, drawling yet confident voice. "What did Creator tell you?"

"She told me enough to know that you're evil. She told me you became greedy for power and tried to kill the king."

"Well, you see, that's not the full story," she absentmindedly twirled her sword's handle between her fingers. "I didn't get blinded by greed. I was just taking back what I was promised. After the king told me he was going to have a child, I accepted it. I was about to step down and become the commander of the army. But then Creator came. She told me to take what was rightfully mine. She said that I deserved to be queen of the galaxy."

"No, she can't have. She would never egg you on like that."

"Oh, but dear, you don't know her. Trust me, I'm on your side. I am trying to save you from her lies. Anyway, then Creator told me to go and challenge the throne. And that ended up with me being thrown into jail-

"And then you grew evil."

"Like I said darling, good and evil matter on perspective. Someone good may not always be good, and someone evil... might have once, been good."

Her voice grew soft at the ending but she cleared her throat and returned to her normal cold self.

"Nice quotes." Said Cosmos, "Do you villains have a website or something, EvilQuotes.com'?"

"What in the living heck are you talking about?"

"Oh nothing, I just said it to throw you off!"

Cosmos used all his willpower to break the chains, and then his green energy caused the purple one to snap.

He lunged at Miss Void once again, but his surroundings changed and he stood in a small room with white walls, and a door with a window on the top.

He ran straight into a wall.

He massaged his head and stared out the window.

Through it he could see a sign that said

GALACTIC JAIL!

A figure came into view. She had long, flowing brown hair and a helmet with two horns extending.

Miss Void smiled apologetically at him and then glided away, leaving him in a prison cell.

"No, no come back!" But it was of no use.

Cosmos slouched against the wall and sat on his small bed.

Chapter 10
Creator loses her Powers

Cosmos tried many ways to escape, but he found himself in a similar predicament as Miss Void had been. His powers were useless against the impenetrable walls.

So he was left with only himself. And as of that moment, that was a pretty bad cell mate.

Once his frustration cleared, all those things that had been at the tip of his mind, but he'd been too busy to focus on them, came back.

And it hit him.

Snogglebrout was dead. He was dead.

And can you guess? Cosmos had been the reason.

He had gotten in the way and distracted him, which got Snogglebrout killed.

No, said a part of his mind, that wasn't your fault. You got hit by a laser, and fell down.

But the laser reminded him of one more thing:

Minister was dead too. The soldier had hit Cosmos and Minister with the laser.

Cosmos survived because of his powers, but Minister hadn't been able to survive.

IT WASN'T YOUR FAULT! Rang the voice in his head.

NO, I'VE GOT THOSE POWERS, I SHOULD HAVE SAVED THEM. Screamed back the other half of his mind.

Why do you think you've got to save everyone?

Because I was trusted with those powers. I was trusted by patients as a doctor, and I let them down.

It wasn't your mistake, okay. Stop hating yourself.

No, you don't understand.

I am literally a part of you.

You still won't understand,

Just then, someone else materialized in the cell.

For a moment, Cosmos was scared it was Miss Void. But it turned out to be Creator.

She just noticed him, and sat down on the bed which had appeared right then.

"Hello?" Cosmos tried to break the ice.

"Hullo." Was the reply.

"What happened?" Asked Cosmos.

Creator did some sort of motion with her fingers, the one she did when she activated her powers, but there was no glow from her palm or wispy strands of blue light emitting form her fingers.

"That lock that Miss Void made, the one on my arm. It drained my powers."

"What?"

"Yes. That lock had some sort of powers in it. I-I'm powerless now. I'm just like a normal human being."

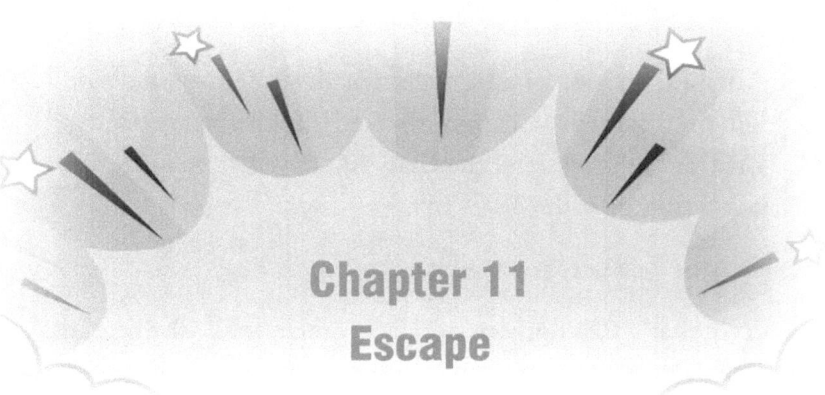

Chapter 11
Escape

Cosmos wasn't exactly in the mood to console her. He had millions of harsh questions formed in his mind, but he didn't ask them so as to make sure she didn't have a complete breakdown.

But, her complaints weren't exactly increasing his sympathy. She talked about being like a normal human as if it was a really crippling disability.

And, as someone who had experienced 'mortal-ness' first hand, Cosmos didn't exactly relate. I mean, what could be so bad about humanity?

"What's wrong with it?" She scoffed, "Oh, nothing, except for the politics, viruses, propaganda, poverty, famines, epidemics, discrimination and overall vulnerability. You think if a normal New Yorker were pitted against a bear, they would win?"

Although he would never admit it to her, she had a point.

After a few days, when Creator finally came to terms with her predicament, Cosmos worked up the nerve to ask Creator the questions that had stuck with him since his conversation with Miss Void.

Creator was hesitant at first.

"No, that's all a figment of her imagination. I... I think all those decades in jail took a toll on her and clouded her judgment."

But Cosmos knew she was lying.

"Tell the truth."

She sighed. She looked as if she would rather stab herself with Miss Void's sword than share the truth with him, but in the end she agreed.

"Yes. I didn't tell you the truth about her. She didn't become greedy for power by herself. I egged her on. I became blinded with pride. Till then, my powers had barely come into use, and when they did, my creations would be asked to help in a battle or a war and then they would be forgotten. I was so proud that one of my works was getting to rule the galaxy. When Miss Void was turned down, she was disappointed, but I fueled her anger. I told her that she deserved to rule the galaxy, and that she should take the position by force."

Cosmos stared at her. All this while, she told her that Miss Void was a power-hungry, evil tyrant.

But he realized that Miss Void was actually ready to step down, but Creator had caused her to get thrown in jail. Which in turn, made her revengeful.

"Cosmos?" She called out.

"Don't talk to me," he said. "Don't say another sentence of lies to me."

"What do you mean."

"I mean, that I won't let you lead me astray like you did with Miss Void."

"What are you talking about, of course I won't. I've changed."

"No, you haven't. You're still filling my mind with false hopes. That I'll be the hero of the galaxy, that I'll be the king."

Without realizing it, Cosmos rose into the air. A green glow radiated out of his body, quickly grew bigger, denser and thicker.

"Cosmos, what's happening?"

Soon, a dome started closing over his head, and now Cosmos head a green orb for a head.

His green energy starting causing the walls of the room to fade away.

"Where are you going?" Asked Creator

The walls completely disappeared. Creator tried to run out of the cell, but an invisible force kept her confined.

"I'm going away from here, from you." said Cosmos.

"Cosmos, what are you doing!"

Cosmos ended up outside the prison wall. Creator tried once again to barge through it, but she was pushed back.

Chapter 12
The Crucial Decision

The battalion of guards stationed outside must have noticed a silhouette that resembled their new prisoner's, so they attacked.

They fired lasers at Cosmos with their space-rifles, but he created a giant wall of energy to ward them off.

"I will let you go peacefully if you stand down!" He said.

"Yeah, right!" Screamed a guard with a scruffy orange beard. "You should step down, or else you'll regret it."

With a couple pushes of his hands, Cosmos sent his barrier of energy crashing down on the guards and they all went scrambling in different directions.

"I gave you a choice," he said.

He activated his powers and a jet-pack like flame came out of his cosmic-gold boots.

"Sayonara!" And with, he zoomed off at top speed.

"She really did that?" Asked Indra.

"Yes, she did." Said Cosmos

Indra sighed heavily. "I can't believe she never told me."

"Well, apparently she didn't tell anyone," said Cosmos.

"No wonder Miss Void's angry at her."

"I don't think 'angry' describes Miss Void's feelings towards Creator."

"True that."

Indra had found Cosmos flying aimlessly in space. He invited him aboard his battleplane, which was made completely of lightning.

Just then, Indra's vahana, Uchchaishravas and his fortune teller, Shrui, walked out of the cockpit. Indra liked to call it the Cracklepit. Indra's friends did not.

"We've reached Earth," said the seven headed horse.

"Well then, my friend, I guess this is good-bye." Said Indra.

"Yeah." Said Cosmos

"If you ever need any help with defeating Miss Void you can call me,"

"Oh no, I'm not going to try and defeat Miss Void,"

"Oh yeah, you're going to plan first. Right?"

"No. I'm going back to live a normal life on Earth."

This statement caused the sky god's eyebrows to rise so much they disappeared into his long brown hair.

"You're not trying to stop Miss Void. You aren't... feeling... you know- empathatic- for her are you? 'Cause I don't care what Creator did, but Miss Void has done some pretty cruel things since she came back."

"Oh no. I don't feel compassionate or anything, it's just, I don't want to get involved in all this."

"Oh and what is 'this'?" Asked Indra, not successful in concealing his anger.

Shrui and Uchchaishravas excused themselves back to the cockpit.

"All this killing and murdering, and evil. I want to get away from it."

"Cosmos, if you leave, the killing and murdering and evil will just run rampant. You are the savior of the galaxy."

"No Indra." He said confirmedly. "I'm not. Now goodbye."

Cosmos opened the door and stepped out into space, hovering above Earth's atmosphere.

"Can I just say one thing," said Indra

"Go on,"

"It's not up to you, you know."

"What isn't?"

The door closed. The battleplane ignited and flew off.

Go back! Screamed a part of his head.

No

You saw how much evil was happening, you need to stop that.

It's neither my fault, nor my responsibility.

Until now it wouldn't have been your fault, but if you don't take action it will be.

And then Shawn realized something. He had nothing to go back down on Earth. His hospital had probably refused to work with him, his house was probably destroyed from the battle, and he would constantly be reminded of his failures.

Minister's and Snogglebrout's bodies were probably still lying in that field, and everyone would know he had been there during the fight.

Going back was probably the easier option. He would much rather fight Miss Void than face what awaited him down there.

Shawn noticed a metal disc zooming towards him.

He noticed it was an empty space-pod. It stopped next to Cosmos and opened the door, with a large banner that said.

In case you're having second-thoughts!

Thank me later,

Indra!

Cosmos laughed out loud, then stepped in.

He placed the banner somewhere else and gripped the steering bar.

"Okay," he sighed, "Let's do this!"

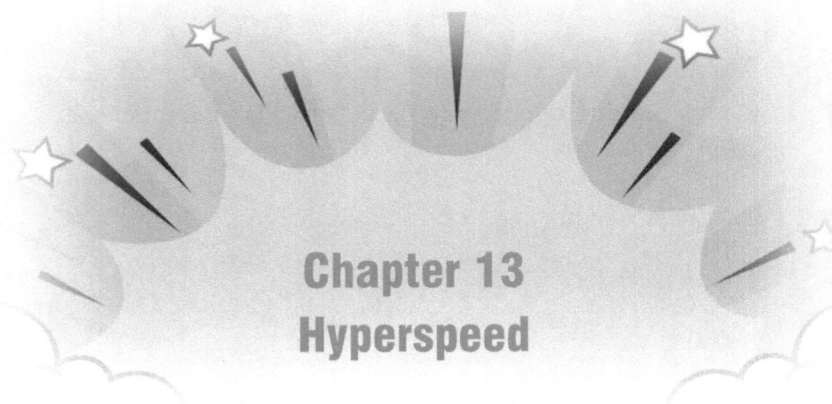

Chapter 13
Hyperspeed

Did you need a license to drive a space-pod?

Because, Cosmos' driving was pretty trashy. He couldn't differentiate between his driving and a roller-coaster ride.

After about 5 minutes of rigorous shaking, he saw a button labelled STABI. Now, that was either a futuristic nickname for stabbing someone or it was a label with half of the word 'stabilizer' erased.

Shawn decided to go with the latter. Once he pressed the button the entire space-pod stopped shaking and he could see where he was driving.

Now the question was, where should he go?

Only one idea came into his mind: Creator.

Yeah, she may have been a jerk, and lied, and the cause of all this but she was really the only person who could guide Cosmos through space.

He had irked off Indra, so he couldn't go there. So, without any map or sense of direction, Shawn set out in search of the Galactic jail.

It seemed to be taking forever, so to speed up the process, he found a little button with the label HYPERSPEED: USE FOR EXTREME SPEED.

So, of course, Shawn pressed that button.

Boy, was that a mistake!

He noticed that the space-pod was going extremely fast.

Soon he couldn't see anything outside, except darkness.

He was moving at the speed of light. He saw multiple beams of different colors zoom past him. For about a few minutes the space pod just drifted limply in that space of colored beams.

He frantically started to look for something that could stop this weird process. Or at least explain it.

Then the space-pod started to slow down and reached normal speed. The beams of color disappeared.

And once the pod came out of the darkness, it was as if Cosmos had flown into a parallel universe.

The looks of some planets had changed, he saw that the portion of Earth which was lush green, had almost turned completely brown.

He realized that he had gone into the future, using the concept of time dilation, which means that when an object is moving extremely fast, it experiences time quicker than when it is at rest. For him only a few seconds passed, but for the rest of the Galaxy, it would have been much more. Maybe even hundreds of centuries.

Cosmos realized that his fuel was running out and he should quickly land somewhere.

He saw a blue planet hovering in orbit and flew towards it.

He flew across the hull of the planet, which was densely covered with ice and water, and spotted a patch of land that may be a continent.

He flew down but pulled the brakes and hovered almost two-hundred feet above the ground.

Once the space-pod's mechanical legs sprung out he landed on the ground. The 'ground' was actually a robust giant sheet of ice, which was this planet's version of continent. The entire planet was made of water, with ice sheets floating on the surface as continents. Cosmos was so immersed in noticing this scenery, that he forgot he had just landed smack in the middle of a town.

The inhabitants of the planet were trembling with fear. Once the doors opened, they all backed away.

"Who are you?" one of them asked him. He was probably the leader. He wore the uniform of the Galactic army, which wasn't a good sign.

"My name... " The army probably knew something about him, and his look hadn't changed so he said, "... is Shawn Stephalla."

Chapter 14
Brim Typhoonian

Did you think you had met everyone who was going to appear in this story? Well I'd like to introduce you to Brim Typhoonian.

You remember Snogglebrout? Brim is his great-great-great-great grandson. And I'm sad to say that the bad luck was passed down during the generations.

Brim sat in his stall, reading a tablet. No, not one of those Samsung S6 Lites. on Neptune, they didn't have books, they had permanent block-like ice-sheets called tablets.

Just then, Bogglebrine walked up to Brim's stall and slammed his fist on the counter.

"Two blue lagoons, Typhoonian," he said with his usual swagger and smirk, "And you better make it quick!"

Is the name Bogglebrine familiar to you. He's the descendant of Banbrine. He constantly bullied Brim.

"I said quick!"

"I'm doing it you-

Bogglebrine grabbed Brim's collar with his muscular arm and slammed him against the wall. His blue scrunched up face was inches away from Brim's small sunken one.

"Did you just talk back to me, you worthless freak?"

"I meant no offence, Bogglebrine," Brim handed him the drink, "Here's your blue lagoon."

"I wanted two."

"I'm making the other one. Here you go."

Bogglebrine walked away.

"Hey, what about my payment?"

"I didn't like your customer service, so I took a free card."

Brim sunk into his seat. This wasn't a new incident. Ever since his childhood, the Neptunians had considered him an outcast because of his ancestor Snogglebrout.

Over the centuries everyone had come to believe that Snogglebrout was a traitor to the galaxy, and that he got what he deserved when Banbrine, the hero of Neptune, killed him.

But Brim's family knew the truth:

Snogglebrout was part of a rebel alliance to counter Miss Void's evil plans. But Banbrine stopped him, acting on behalf of Miss Void.

The whole of Neptune knew Snogglebrout and Banbrine, the traitor and the savior.

But to Brim, Snogglebrout was the greatest hero ever. He stood up to tyranny and malice, but died a martyr.

It was Brim's dream that he would one day do something great to follow in Snogglebrout's footsteps, but he neither had his ancestor's strength nor his resilience.

And he would rather hug Bogglebrine than admit it but Brim sometimes wondered if he really was as good-for-nothing and worthless as the townspeople thought him to be.

After an hour, during every shop's mandatory lunch-break, Brim stepped out of his stall and saw a weird sight.

A metal disc was landing in their town. No, it was a space-pod. The UFO's mechanical legs sprung out and landed on the ice.

Slowly after, the door opened, and a being walked out. He wore beige armor with blue lights and a purple triangular shape.

He had a green ball for a head and wore a flowing red cape.

"Who are you?" Asked one of the Neptunians.

"My name… " he paused and bit back something, "… is Shawn Stephalla."

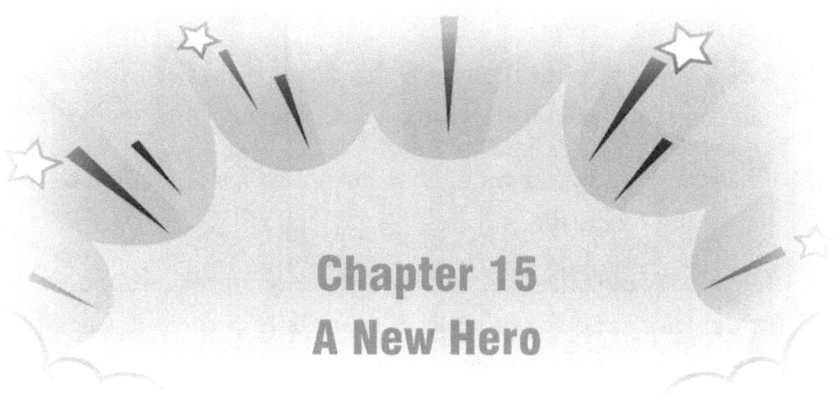

Chapter 15
A New Hero

The first thing Cosmos noticed was the people. They were almost exactly how aliens were depicted on Earth, except they were a bit more human-like. They wore metal fabrics and shorts that were gold in color, and had light blue skin. Their average height was 5'8 and they all had brown hair.

But one Neptunian stood out to him. He stood in the back of the crowd but was short enough to stand out and catch Cosmos' attention.

Then the leader, the one with the Galactic-Army uniform said,

"You don't look like a normal being, Sewalla, would you care to explain?" His tone immediately made Cosmos dislike him.

"My name's not Sewalla, its Stephalla, and I look weird cause I'm from a different... " he would have said that he was from Earth but then he realized that a soldier of the galactic army must have visited Earth once.

That caused another thought to rush into his head: what happened to Earth?

Did Miss Void take over and spread her tyranny there too, or did Indra and the other gods manage to protect it. But he thought he should deal with the situation at present.

"... galaxy. I'm from a different galaxy."

In his brain he thought,

What the heck did I just say?

So you could just imagine the reaction on the Neptunians face.

"Oh, then, welcome to Toirstarin."

"Wait, what?"

"Toirstarin, it's the name of our town."

"No, I mean, I'm from a different galaxy, and you didn't have any reaction?"

"Yeah, I didn't. Now do you want to come in or not?"

The first thing Bogglebrine (the leader) did was take Cosmos to a drink stall. And there, he saw that short blue Neptunian.

"One blue lagoon for our kind guest here Brim, and you better make it quick this time." "All right," squeaked Brim. He got to work.

"Why were you so rude to him?"

"Who? Oh, Brim. He's a freak."

That wasn't a normal reply.

"Why?"

"Because he's the descendant of a damn traitor that's why!"

"Traitor?" Asked Cosmos.

"Yeah," said Bogglebrine, "Snogglebrout. The cursed wretch put a stain on his position as chief of the army and went and conspired to kill Miss Void, our ruler."

If Cosmos had his way, he would have ripped Bogglebrine apart limb for limb and mutilated his body with cosmic energy but he had to keep his calm. He may be a Celestial, but he was pretty sure if he killed one soldier, thousands more would come rushing to the spot. "Oh really! But what if you don't know the full story?"

For some reason, Brim's eyebrows shot up at this reply and disappeared into his long wiry hair. Then he handed them the drink. "Your drink."

"We're in the middle of a discussion here, you half-wit!" Said Bogglebrine, but he still took a sip from the drink.

Even though it was supposed to be for Cosmos. But that wasn't the problem.

And for some reason, this made something in Cosmos' brain snap.

Why did Bogglebrine bully Brim so much? That poor kid didn't do anything to him.

"Why do you need to be so rude to him?" Asked Cosmos.

"Don't tell me you're standing up for him, he's just a good-for-nothing weirdo."

"Why? Because he's descended from an actual hero and not a fake puppet for Miss Void?"

"Did you just call my ancestor a puppet?"

"Oh, I have a lot of other names for him,"

"Okay, just who the heck do you think you are?!"

"I'm the guy who's going to give you the same fate Snogglebrout got if you don't shut up!"

At that point Brim piped up, "I'm not a kid. I've just got really low height!"

But the look on Bogglebrine's face spoke all of his emotions.

"Wait a minute. You're that Celestial who went missing after breaking out of the galactic jail!"

"Yes. I am."

Suddenly, Bogglebrine's expression changed. He pulled out a remote-like thing from his uniform's pocket and pressed a large blue button. Soon, an army of soldiers surrounded them.

Then Bogglebrine pressed a button that played something that sounded like a calling ringtone.

"What is it?" Asked a cold, confident voice. It was a woman's.

"My Mistress, I found a treat for you,"

"What is it?"

"Oh, you will absolutely love it!"

"Get to the point, Boggled-brain!"

He muttered something like, 'it's Bogglebrine'.

"Did you just talk back to me, you insolent fool?"

For some unknown reason, Brim snickered silently at this.

Bogglebrine glared at him. "No, my mistress."

"Then get to the darn point!"

"Yes, my mistress, I'll cut it short."

"You better."

" After all your years of hard and earnest effort, I found Cosmos." There was silence from the other end. Then a chuckle.

"Keep him there, I'm coming."

She disconnected.

"You heard the mistress! Capture him!"

The soldiers started advancing towards him.

"Don't even think about it," said Cosmos. He activated his power in his hand and shot a wide arc, causing the entire front row to fall on their backs, clutching their chest.

The others activated their Space-Ray Blaster, but Cosmos sent them scrambling with two more blasts. Then he walked menacingly towards Bogglebrine.

"Back off and surrender! Y-You don't know who you're messing with!" Stammered the Neptunian.

Bogglebrine loaded his space-ray blaster.

But the anger towards him in Cosmos' head was so profound, that he activated a sort of mental power and tossed the gun into another shop without even touching it.

Cosmos grabbed Bogglebrine by the collar and threw him over. Then he created a big green oval of energy, and pushed Bogglebrine inside. The latter tried to barge out but found that whenever his skin came in contact with the energy, he got a jolt in his stomach.

"Enjoy, Boggled-Brain!" Said Cosmos. Then he started to fly away, towards his space-pod but when he reached he found another group of soldiers had demolished it.

The blue skinned, muscular commandos smirked. Then they aimed their Space-Ray Blasters.

Cosmos stunned them each one by one. The second came running after the first fell to his knees, and the third and fourth ran away in fear after the second one got tossed with a wispy ball of green energy hovering over his head.

Then Cosmos realised something. He didn't need a space-pod to get out of there, in fact he had something much quicker, but only advanced Celestials could perform that task. He had seen Miss Void do it when she trapped him in the cell.

Cosmos focused all his power on one thought: to summon a transportation beam. A transportation beam is something a Celestial can summon when they need to move from a specific spot to another.

Sure enough, a green beam the width of a school bus formed in the sky and was about to crash on the ground.

Cosmos was almost about to let it transport him, when he saw the kid from the stall running towards him.

"Wait, sir Cosmos!" He called out. "Take this!"

Brim was being chased by two bulky soldiers, and his short height and skinniness let him slip away from tight corners faster. Brim held out a remote in his hand.

Cosmos moved away from the beam. While holding out one hand towards the beam to will it not to disappear, he shot down the other soldiers with his other hand.

Brim came panting towards him, and held out the remote.

"This is Bogglebrine's communication device, if you take it with you, he won't be able to call Miss Void."

"Thanks kid-sorry, Brim."

"Also, I need to ask a favor,"

"Go on,"

"Can I join you?"

"What do you mean?"

"Can I join you, to defeat Miss Void?"

"Umm, it'll be dangerous-

"It's okay. They'll arrest me for helping you anyway."

Cosmos saw that they needed to escape quickly.

"Okay, fine. But if anything happens to you, I won't be held responsible."

Cosmos held up his arm, and willed the beam to teleport them.

For a second, he only saw white, then his vision slowly came back to him.

He was standing on hard, grey rocky ground. On his left was a giant black compound he recognized as the Galactic Jail.

On his right was Brim. He staggered around a bit until he held on to a pillar with a giant red button. The problem was that he leaned on the button, and pressed it.

Immediately, an alarm went off, and several space-pods, modified with large cannon like guns extending out of the legs, surrounded them.

"They've improved security," Cosmos noted.

Chapter 16
An Epic Dogfight

When the space-pods started firing, Cosmos created a green shield to protect him and Brim. He then gave the shield destructive powers and sent it flying at the space-pods. One pod crashed on the ground while the other got away. Unfortunately, three more space-pods appeared. They fired lasers so fast that Cosmos didn't have time to concentrate on creating another shield.

He grabbed Brim's arm and lead him into the crashed space-pod. Cosmos made the pilot float out and buckled himself into the pilot's seat.

"I'd suggest you hold on to those rails," he told Brim.

Brim did as told. He was reconsidering joining this quest, but then he reminded himself of the reason why he volunteered. It was the perfect chance to try and achieve his goal.

He wanted to see his ancestor, Snogglebrout, no longer treated like a traitor. He wanted to exact revenge on Miss Void for killing him and defaming him. With Cosmos' help, he could finally kill Miss Void, and once again bring glory to his family's name.

But he had to focus on the task at hand. First, he had to focus on... wait, why had they come here?

That's what he asked Cosmos.

"To rescue Creator," was the reply.

"The being that Miss Void trapped. The one that created you and her?"

"Yes, but she also... " Cosmos hesitated. "Nothing."

"What happened?"

"I told you, nothing-OH MY GOD!"

A huge missile narrowly missed them and exploded in a huge crater.

"Let's focus on the task at hand-getting into the jail. But for that, we've got to get past these space-pods."

The second space-pod started shooting at them from its cannon-gun.

"And I guess we'll have to fight fire with fire," said Cosmos, "Literally."

He pressed a few buttons on the control panel, and soon enough, a cannon sprouted out of their space-pod's leg.

"Eat this!" Cosmos vigorously pressed a blue button and the cannon started shooting lasers at the space-pods.

Brim noticed a large button on the control panel at the back. He walked towards it and saw that it said

SUPER DESTRUCTIVE MISSILE: ONLY USE IN EMERGENCY

Cosmos fired continuously and tried some other weapons. There was one that sent a sonic soundwave radiating out of the space-pod, and the other pilots covered their ears.

"Ha!" he exclaimed. He pressed a small green button and moved around with a joystick.

The cannon re-loaded and fired an extremely destructive beam that hit a space-pod and caused it to crash into the one next to it.

The pilot in the other space-pod also tried to aim a missile at them but Cosmos saw him and hit him with the 'Destructo-Beam.'

"Please don't call it that," said Brim.

The last space-pod activated a shield around itself. No amount of beams penetrated that shield, and there was no damage.

"There is one option," said Brim

"What?"

Brim told him about the super destructive missile.

"Well what are we waiting for, use it!"

"Okay," Brim pressed the button.

"There's a little text that says you control it with the joystick."

"Okay." Cosmos moved the joystick but the missile didn't launch. "It's not happening. Can you go and check?"

"Okay."

The moment Brim opened the door and looked down, he regretted it. They were two-hundred feet above the ground!

Brim couldn't see anything so he carefully placed a leg on the cannon, and then balanced his whole body on.

The cannon then sprouted a missile from a mechanical compartment below it.

To check further, Brim looked down to see, but slipped.

Thankfully he held onto a bar that was attached to the missile. But then the situation worsened. A timer on the missile started counting.

10.

Oh no. Brim had to get off, or he would go flying with the missile. But there was no way to. If he tried, he would fall down from two-hundred feet.

7

6

5

4

3

2

This is it, he thought, I'm gonna die.

1

0.

The missile blasted forward with extreme speed. Brim barely registered the strong smell of the missile's fuel, which smelled almost like petroleum. His wiry hair was almost peeled off as the missile cut through the air.

Brim saw Cosmos from the window and saw the latter mouthing something along the lines of, 'Let go!'

The missile was almost about to hit the shield, and the moment it would come in contact with the shield, it would explode.

So Brim let go.

The funny thing was he fell with almost as much speed as the missile launched. Brim thought for sure he was going to die, but then he saw Cosmos' space-pod wheel around, and he had managed to open a sun-roof.

Cosmos' timing was so impeccable that Brim fell straight into the pod.

The space-pod came to a stop and hovered in the air.

Brim held onto the pole and placed a hand over his thumping heart.

Cosmos' green orb of a head seemed to retract into his green skin.

Beneath it was a human face, with messy dirty blonde hair, spectacles, and a concerned look.

"Are you okay?"

"Yes. My hands are just hurting from holding on the bar so tight."

Cosmos gave a sigh of relief.

"Are you sure you still want to continue on this mission, because it's going to get a hundred times more dangerous from now on."

Brim thought it over in his head, but he knew his answer from the start.

"Heck yeah!"

Chapter 17
Miss Void Appears. Again. Hooray

Dr. Cosmos landed the space-pod on the ground.

"C'mon, let's get out of here," said Cosmos as he opened the door hatch and led Brim out. They flew to the floor which Cosmos and Creator were imprisoned on. Cosmos blasted the wall to shambles, and they heard the startled noise someone makes when they're woken up from sleep abruptly.

They saw a young woman (she looked young, she was actually thousands of years old) with multicolored hair and an orange T-shirt from Earth, above it was a gold-armor chest-plate.

"Hello Creator," said Cosmos.

Creator seemed in shock for a while, then she came to her senses and a smile broke across her face.

"H-Hello Shawn!" She said.

"Shawn?" Brim inquired, "That's your actual name?"

"Yes. It used to be," said Cosmos. "Not anymore, I've put Shawn Stephalla past me."

"What do you mean?"

"-Excuse me, umm, who's this?" Creator asked, pointing at Brim.

"He's Brim. He's from Neptune."

"Does he have any powers?"

"In a sense, yes."

"You mean he doesn't. Why did you bring him along?"

"Oh, you don't know how big of an asset he is. He may not look like much, but trust me, he can help. Do you know he just flew on a missile?"

"What?"

"Yeah, and he escaped the Galactic soldiers on Neptune to help me."

Cosmos saw his praise of Brim had caused a small smile to appear on the latter's face. He felt he owed to Brim, seeing as he had just risked his life. He had been the one to ask Brim to go check on the missile, and thus caused him to almost die.

But Cosmos admired Brim's determination, even after such a scary incident, he still wanted to continue on the mission. Cosmos had thought, for a second, that Brim was going to die, and that reminded him of all the people that had died on his watch.

The old lady, Minister, Snogglebrout.

He remembered Brim was Snogglebrout's descendant, and that just made him want to protect him even more.

After Creator heard everything about Brim, they all went back into the space-pod.

But before Cosmos was about to start the engine, a massive purple beam struck the ground.

It was like Cosmos' green transportation beam, but purple, and for some reason it looked more sinister.

The beam retracted into the sky to reveal a feminine figure, wearing a dark green suit, a green cape and a helmet with two metal horns. In her hand, she held a sword with the illusion of dust on the tip.

She looked up, and Cosmos felt a chill down his spine.

An evil smile spread across Miss Void's sharp face.

Chapter 18
Miss Void's Prisoner

"I was wondering where you had disappeared, Cosmos," Miss Void said.

In her mind, Miss Void chuckled at his almost comical name. But she didn't let the emotion spread onto her face, so as to not let any of them think, for a minute, that she wasn't serious about this situation.

She wanted to send shivers of terror down their spines, and show them that she was the queen of the galaxy. No one could take that from her.

But most importantly, she wanted to get her hands on that wretched liar.

Creator. The name made you think of a heroic, caring being. But in reality, she was a selfish, vain, deceiver.

Everyone saw what Miss Void did, how she attempted to take the throne, but they never saw that behind all that was one two-faced jerk of a Celestial.

Sure, she had attempted to overthrow the king, but did anyone say anything to Creator for implanting those ideas in her head.

And for that injustice, Miss Void was going to kill her. She had been kind to only imprison her, and take away her powers. But now Creator was going to pay for her atrocities.

The moment Miss Void got past Cosmos she would detain Creator and send her to the Galactic Palace, where she would be killed in a public execution.

But she had to focus on the first part: getting past Cosmos. She had no intention to kill him, but he was like a little splinter that, no matter how many times you tried, wouldn't be removed.

"I won't let you hurt Creator, or Brim," said Cosmos.

"Brim?" Asked Miss Void. "What is Brim?"

Then she noticed a little Neptunian, who sat inside the pod, petrified. His teeth were chattering in fear.

"I-I'm Brim." He managed to say.

"Well Brim," said Miss Void, in a tone that was not exactly menacing, "I'll give you an offer. Come and join me. No need to hang around with that liar. I will make you the chief of the galactic army. Tell you what, Cosmos, I'll give you the same. You can be my most important Minister!"

"Ha!" Said Cosmos. "Join you? No way in hell!"

Miss Void had expected him to say something like that.

"You're a gone case, Cosmos," said Miss Void, "And you Brim?"

"What he said," said the Neptunian, who seemed to have found a sort of disgust and contempt in his voice. "No way in hell!"

Miss Void sighed. She had to give it to them, they were stubborn.

Miss Void gripped her sword and lit up her purple energy in her hand.

"Then either you step out of my way," she blasted open the door of the space-pod, "or you get disintegrated!"

She ran towards the space-pod but Cosmos flew out and shot multiple balls of energy at her. She dodged.

Miss Void and Cosmos both shot at the same time, and their flares of energy met together.

Now they were locked in something called a Celestial Tangle. If any Celestial withdrew, or their energy power reduced, the combined force of theirs and the other's energy would hit them in an extremely destructive blast.

But Miss Void had a trick up her sleeve. This was the perfect opportunity. She could trap Cosmos in another dimension.

Miss Void used her index finger and drew a figure resembling Cosmos using wispy purple energy.

Then she used her mental powers and grew it to his actual size.

A look of confusion appeared on Cosmos' face.

She withdrew her hand and stepped aside. The combined energy hit the Galactic jail's pillar and it crumbled.

Then, before Cosmos could react, she pushed his drawing towards him and the energy dissolved into him.

Then, slowly, he faded away.

In the space-pod, Brim and Creator said in unison, "What did you do!"

Miss Void created an oval shape with purple energy around the space-pod, and trapped the pod, and its passengers inside.

"Your precious hero is now trapped in the fourth dimension," Miss Void summoned her transportation beam and pushed the trapped space-pod into the beam. Then she ran towards the beam, and willed it to take her to Galactic palace.

For a moment she saw white, then she landed in the galactic palace, inside the Sun.

Creator was now completely at Miss Void's mercy, and Cosmos was not going to return anytime soon.

Chapter 19
The God of the Sky Comes to Help

If there was anything worse than almost dying on a missile, it was being captured by the evilest person in the galaxy.

But, unlike the other times Brim had been stuck in an extremely bad situation, and believe me it was a lot of times, Brim didn't lose hope.

When Bogglebrine bullied him, he used to have a sense to fight back. However, when Bogglebrine beat him up afterwards, Brim decided to give up.

However, that was not the case here. Brim had, in the first few seconds, looked at Miss Void with fear, but afterwards, he remembered how she had caused the death of Snogglebrout, and regained his fury, and desire for revenge.

Earlier, if Brim had been caught like this, he would have given up hope and apologized to Miss Void. But now, the only thing he could still think of was slicing off the tyrant's neck.

But, there was still the fact that he was scrawny, weak, below-height, and not very courageous.

So he needed help. He joined Cosmos as he thought Cosmos would surely be of physical help to kill Miss Void.

But now Cosmos was trapped in another dimension. And Creator would be of no use.

However, help soon arrived.

Once they reached the Sun, and were about to enter through the flames of gas, yellow lighting flashed outside.

Brim turned and saw huge tendrils of electricity emitting out of a being that was floating in space, and held a huge, crackling lightning bolt in his right hand.

"Miss Void," called out the being, "You have been wise to not trespass on the territory of the gods till now. But if you advance further with my friend, you will face the wrath of Lord Indra."

The king of Gods directed all his electricity towards the space-pod.

The space-pod rattled and shook violently as Indra flew towards it.

Miss Void got up from her seat in the front and gripped her sword.

Soon she was outside.

Brim heard her say,

"I am the queen of this galaxy, and I will bow to no one. I do not wish to fight you mighty Indra, but if you won't leave I will be left with no choice."

Indra gave a sardonic chuckle. "You say that as if you think you will be able to win against me."

Miss Void smirked evilly. "Is that a challenge?"

"No," said Lord Indra. Then his whole body transformed into pure electricity, and he rapidly grew to ten times his normal size. "It's an ultimatum."

The lord of weather flew towards Miss Void, who held her sword in a ready-to-strike pose, and lit up her signature purple energy in her left hand.

However, she was not given a chance to attack.

Lord Indra picked her up with his right hand, and tossed her away.

Then he returned to his normal size and materialized in the space-pod.

The pilot took one look at him and jumped out the door.

Indra then electrocuted Creator and Brim's chains and cause them to break.

"Indra. Thank god!" Said Creator.

"You're welcome!" Lord Indra did a mock bow. "Where's Cosmos?"

"He's trapped in the fourth dimension," said Brim.

"Sorry who are you again, I don't think I've seen you before?" Asked Indra.

"He's Brim. Cosmos' friend." Said Creator.

Then Brim saw a purple blur zooming towards the space-pod, which was on auto-pilot.

"Miss Void's coming back." Creator said firmly.

"Indra," Creator turned towards him, "Can you rescue Cosmos from the fourth dimension."

Indra stared at her incredulously.

"Of course I can!"

"Great then, you go and-

"Creator are you crazy, of course I can't!"

"But you just said-

"Ever heard of sarcasm?"

Creator sighed.

"Are you sure it's not possible?"

"Well, it has not been attempted many times before. I could ask for help from Brahma, who resides in the fifth dimension of Multiverses, Vishnu, who looks over the death and birth of each of those Brahmas, or maybe Shiva, the ultimate god-

"Wait a minute," said Brim, "I thought you were the most powerful god."

"Me? I wish! I am just the king of the heavens-

"That's the ultimate position isn't it?"

"No. There are Gods much more powerful than me. There is Brahma, who I mentioned. There is a different Brahma in each universe. Then there is Vishnu who oversees the prosperity of each Brahma's universe. And then there is Shiva, the destroyer, also known as the God of Gods! All these multiple universes make the Multiverse, or, the Karna Ocean-

"Umm, sorry to interrupt your education, but Miss Void is almost here," said Creator. "Please, Indra, if it's possible, can you bring Cosmos back?"

"Okay," said Indra. "I'll go and find Cosmos but I can't leave you here without any support so...

Indra took a bolt of lightning and molded it into something that resembled a sword.

"Brim Typhoonian," he said and handed the sword to him, "Use this to keep Miss Void at bay until I return with Cosmos."

Miss Void had finally reached and practically glided towards them. She held her sword high, ready to strike at Indra- or maybe she was aiming for Creator.

But Lord Indra dissolved into electricity at that moment so Miss Void was about to slice Creator's neck off, but Brim blocked her with the lightning sword.

"Step aside, Neptunian," Miss Void threatened.

"No." Said Brim. For the record, he had no idea where he was getting this much confidence. "I won't!"

"Then I will have no choice but to kill you,"

"Believe me Miss Void," At this point Brim felt like a totally new person, fueled by anger. "I won't die without killing you first."

Chapter 20
The Worst Kind of Prison

Do you know about white-torture prison cells?

It's specially designed to make a prisoner go mad. They're trapped in this room, which is completely white. The toilet, walls, bed, even their clothes, are all white.

And after a few weeks, they go insane.

Well, Cosmos found himself in almost the same predicament. He was trapped in the fourth dimension. He could see everything that happened around him, but it was as if he was an NPC (non-playable characters) in a badly-designed video game.

Nothing he did had any affect in the world he was seeing. If he blasted anything with energy, the energy would just disappear.

In fact, he was standing with Brim, Creator and Indra right there, but it was as if he was viewing a VR movie.

He tried shooting at Miss Void but nothing happened.

His shots just went past her.

Being in that situation was ten times worse than if he was actually there. If he was actually there, he would have the mental satisfaction of knowing that he can try to change what was going to happen.

Now, he was confined in this transparent trap.

Miss Void sure was wicked. She could have easily killed him with that shot, but she chose to put him through this torture. To see his friends in the jaws of danger and not be able to do anything about it.

Then he realized something ten times worse. He was literally living his doubts.

Ever since that craniotomy went wrong, Shawn had been doubting himself, even hating himself sometimes.

He used to think that he was useless, that he didn't deserve all those awards he got.

Then he was made a Celestial. And then he had thought, that now the entire galaxy's freedom depended on him. A hopeless, self-doubting moron.

And then Snogglebrout and Minister got killed. And it was his fault.

His self-hatred came hurtling back towards him like a weaponized boomerang.

But then he met Miss Void, and after recovering from the initial chill down his spine, he realized that someone had to save this galaxy.

Then he found out the truth about Creator, the one being he respected the most. He realized that both Creator and Miss Void were somewhat the same in their own ways, though Creator still had some of her morals.

And then he went five-hundred years into the future. He met Brim, and was instantly reminded of Snogglebrout.

He made a silent vow to himself that he would protect Brim from everything he could.

He fought against Bogglebrine. And when Brim launched off with that missile, Cosmos was scared that, like his ancestor, Brim would die on Cosmos' watch.

And now he was trapped in this different dimension.

It was like one giant taunt from Miss Void. And he realized that, whatever ounce of empathy he once had for her, was gone.

He still understood that Creator had been a jerk, but he was sure Miss Void had her power-hungry, malicious, wicked persona in her from the start. All she had needed was a little push.

And the villain inside her would awaken.

When Indra disappeared into electricity to get Cosmos back, the latter felt like shouting,

"I'M RIGHT HERE!"

And then tendrils of electricity materialized In front of Cosmos and started forming the shape of a man.

And Lord Indra was there. But he was clutching his eyes.

"Ah! I can't see!" He said.

"What?" Asked Cosmos. "Why can't you see?"

"Do you know how difficult it is, even for a god, to materialize into the fourth dimension with ease. It causes a normal person to turn non-existent. I just hope I'm not blinded forever. Yeah, there we go!"

He removed his hand and blinked a few times.

"Right let's get you out of here," said the Lord of the sky, weather, and lightning.

"But how?" Asked Cosmos.

Indra took in a deep breath. "Okay, short version-it's a little more difficult than arriving."

"So you mean next to impossible?"

"Ye... ah."

"All right, tell me how,"

"So you know that transportation-beam-thingy you do?"

"Yes,"

"Well, you need to do that, but at the same time, I need to create my own transportation beam. Then we need to merge the two. And then, we might just have a chance of getting out of here."

"What do you mean, 'might'?"

"Well 'might' is a modal verb used to express the possibility that something will happen or be done, or that something is true although not very like-

"I'm sorry, when did you turn into the Cambridge Dictionary?"

"Sorry, I got side-tracked."

"And I wasn't asking the definition of might, I was asking if you actually know that this will work?"

There was silence.

"Yesn't?"

"Alright, how do even know that word?"

"Just because I'm a god, doesn't mean I'm

 not updated."

Cosmos sighed.

"Well, it's worth a shot."

Cosmos focused his will, and a green transportation beam appeared.

Indra raised his fist up and a blue beam made of electric bolts appeared.

" We run into it on three." Said Cosmos

"Wait, by 'on three' do you mean after three, or on three?"

"After,"

"All right."

Cosmos willed the beam to move with his hands, and so did Indra to his.

Soon, the two massive beams were in close proximity to each other, then they automatically merged together as if they were pulled by a magnetic force.

"One," Said Cosmos.

"Two," said Indra.

"Three!" The both said in unison.

They both ran towards the merged green beam with flickering bolts of electricity and got pulled by it.

But then they got shoved back and landed on their backs.

"Damn it!" Indra screamed.

Cosmos noticed that Indra's portion of the beam had disappeared, but his part was still there.

Cosmos thought if he could focus on all of his power and transfer it into this beam, he could get Indra out.

It would probably drain him out, but at least Indra could get out and help Brim and Creator.

So Cosmos focused all of his energy, channeled all his emotions towards the beam, and making it stronger.

And he could just feel it in his nerves, that it worked.

"Indra, try again,"

Indra got up and examined the green beam.

"Are you sure it'll work?"

"Yesn't."

Indra chuckled. "You are cheeky, I'll give you that."

Indra stepped into the beam and so did Cosmos.

They both raised their hand into the air and willed it.

Please work, Cosmos prayed.

And it did.

Cosmos saw that everything his eyes were passing down to his brain, all those images, just shattered into a million pieces.

And he saw everything clearly. He once again felt like he was actually existing in the environment he was seeing.

And then he realized, that he made it. He had hoped his powers would make the beam strong enough to break Indra out, but he had made it so powerful that it didn't drain his powers and still transported both of them.

And after realizing that, Cosmos felt a wave of happiness fall over him.

He realized that he was capable enough, if not more, to defeat Miss Void. He could save the galaxy.

Then he saw Brim and Miss Void next to each other. Brim was sword-fighting Miss Void with his lightning sword.

Cosmos knew that Brim could handle himself in that situation, but he wasn't going to sit back.

He lit up his hand with his green energy, activated the green orb around his head, and charged.

Chapter 21
The Neptunian and The Tyrant

Brim's mind was swirling with ideas and emotions so much, that if every single emotion of his represented a color, his mind would be a Jackson Pollock painting.

He noticed that he had this habit in him, where his attitude would constantly go back and forth. He had decided to ignore Bogglebrine's bullying, but then Cosmos came along and he rebelled against the former.

Then he made up his mind that he would take revenge on Miss Void. But then he got captured and decided to apologize his way out of it. But then Indra appeared and Brim decided to fight. And the moment Miss Void challenged him to a duel, he thought,

What the heck am I thinking?

But then, surprisingly, he turned out to be good at sword-fighting, and decided that he would finish Miss Void once and for all. He never practiced it but the movements came naturally to him, as if they were in his genes.

Miss Void thrust, but Brim blocked. He turned his head and saw that Creator had found a space-ray blaster and had started shooting off the soldiers one by one. He didn't know what happened between Cosmos and Creator, but he had decided to let it be.

Miss Void sent a blast of energy at him, jerking him back to reality, and he dodged.

Miss Void had shifted her method of attacking from her sword to her shots, and, while dodging her shots, Brim came up close to her and slashed a wide arc.

Miss Void winced when the lightning sword tore through her sleeve and slashed her left arm, leaving a little electric tingling in the area.

Miss Void's left arm was damaged, so she couldn't fire any energy flares. Her only resort now was to fight through her sword.

"If that's how you want it to be Neptunian," she said, panting.

She charged and they engaged in a rapid exchange of thrusts, blocks, and parries.

From afar, it looked like a lightsaber battle.

They both stepped away from each other to rest their arms.

Brim knew it was now or never. If he failed now, he wouldn't just be jailed, he would turn into dust. Forever.

Just then, a spectacle distracted both him and Miss Void.

He heard the sound of an explosion.

Brim saw a gigantic green burst of energy. And from it a being burst forward.

It was Cosmos. The latter activated the green orb that appeared on his head whenever he went into battle. He lit up his signature green energy and posed backwards like an angry bull ready to charge.

And charge he did.

Miss Void stood watching, with one limp arm, a sword dangling from about three fingers on her right arm, and a dumb-struck expression.

Cosmos willed his energy to form the shape of a giant green fist. Then he flew towards Miss Void at extreme speed.

His energy-fist grew as he charged and soon was bigger than Miss Void. It punched Miss Void and caused her to go flying.

She crashed on a nearby asteroid on her back. Then she regained her senses and stood up. She threw her sword aside and lit up her energy.

"It seems there is no way to get rid of you," she said, "So then. Let's fight. No weapons. No extra help. Just you and me. Winner takes all, Loser takes none. And by none I mean death!"

"Choose your terms wisely Miss Void, you are the one with the injured arm after all! You can still surrender"

"The arm is just a mere hindrance."

"Well then," said Cosmos, "So be it. But don't say I didn't give you a chance to surrender."

He charged towards the asteroid, and at the same time Miss Void leaped into the air. She aimed her right arm at her and shot her flare of energy. At the same time, Cosmos did the same.

Their flares met at the same point, causing a Celestial Triangle, and they both needed to back theirs up with more energy. If any one of their energy reduced, the combined force would hit the other with life-threatening destructive power.

Chapter 22
The Duel of the Celestials

For at least a minute, the two stood there. Brim, Creator and Indra didn't get involved in the fight as it was supposed to be only between Cosmos and Miss Void. It looked insanely epic from afar.

Then, Cosmos' energy overpowered Miss Void's and she was sent crashing down to the asteroid. Again. Her helmet with the metal horns fell of her head and rolled away, to reveal her brown hair, which was wrapped in a tight bun.

Cosmos finally thought that he had a chance to win.

He landed on the asteroid in a perfect-superhero pose and jumped, making the energy-fist again. He punched Miss Void once again, causing her to get flattened down on the ground inside a newly-formed crater. Her bun loosened and her brown hair flew into her face.

Cosmos landed on the ground again and ran up to Miss Void. He was about to hit her with another flare of energy.

But then Miss Void stretched out her right hand, and her sword came flying into it.

She gripped her sword tightly. Cosmos was already going to land next to her and his arms were busy so he couldn't defend himself.

The moment he was close enough, Miss Void plunged the sword through his armor and into his stomach.

A painful expression appeared on his face. He fell on his knees. He didn't turn into dust as his Celestial life-force would absorb the damage. But it still de-mobilized him.

Miss Void yanked the sword out.

"You... You said no weapons," said Cosmos weakly.

"Oh well," she said in a taunting voice, "I guess I lied."

Cosmos rested on his back, clutching the wound.

He saw Brim activate his lightning sword. Indra also charged at Miss Void.

But she struck down Brim with a blast of energy and trapped Indra in a purple bubble. Much like the one Cosmos trapped Bogglebrine in.

Miss Void got up again. She tossed her head to remove the hair that stuck to her forehead after being set loose from its tight bun, and wore the helmet that had fallen down.

"I told you Cosmos," she said. There wasn't even a mocking tone in her voice any more. All that was left was plain, old evil. "You could have joined me. But you chose to defend Creator."

"At least... " Cosmos managed to say, "At least I'm on the right side."

Miss Void gave a fake chuckle. "The right side. Do you know what I think about the right side? I think that the so called 'right' side is just the side of the winner. History is written by the winner after all. It doesn't matter if they are good or bad. It matters if they won. Who knows? A hundred years from now, people will adore me as a hero and remember you as a villain."

"That's where you're wrong," said Cosmos, pressing his hand against the wound. "History may be written according to the victor, but it doesn't matter what history says. It matters what the people believe. On the whole of Neptune, Snogglebrout and his entire family were regarded upon as traitors, but Brim still remembered Snogglebrout's great deeds, and his sacrifice. A hundred years from now, most people might worship you as a hero, out of respect or fear I don't know, but there will always be one person that knows what true greatness is."

Miss Void looked taken aback, but then her usual determined, malicious face returned.

"Enough talking. Let's put an end to you."

She raised her hands and aimed at him, but then Cosmos heard the sound of lasers being shot.

Miss Void hunched over, lost balance, and fell over. Standing behind her was a woman in an orange polo shirt, over which she wore gold-armor, holding a space-ray blaster which was still smoking at the tip.

"No," said Creator. "The time has come, to put an end to you."

Chapter 23
Creator's Sacrifice

Creator trudged towards Miss Void, who was hunched over, panting.

"I know what I did to you was wrong," said Creator, "I influenced you to take the throne by force. And you got captured. I am responsible for that. But my actions are no justification for your unjust rule. For the terror you have inflicted upon the galaxy. I used to make people believe you are evil just so they would defend me from you, but now? I truly believe you are."

Miss Void scoffed. "Like I care what you think."

"I am sorry." Said Creator. "About your capture."

She was so just five inches away from Miss Void.

"I don't need your apology," said Miss Void. "I need to see your body turned into dust!"

Creator disregarded that comment.

Creator looked at Miss Void, and felt a surge of sympathy. She decided to at least try to give her a second chance.

Creator extended her hand. "You can still back down. We'll let you live."

A happy smile appeared on Miss Void's face, though it looked kind of fake.

She grabbed Creator's hand and got up.

"That's so sweet of you!" She said.

Miss Void stabbed Creator in her leg. Then she yanked it out.

"But no thank you!"

A look of surprise washed over Creator's face. She hurried over to Cosmos and held his hand. The latter looked extremely surprised.

Soon, a blue energy passed from Creator's hand to his, and Cosmos' wound healed. He got up and looked in the best of shape. Meanwhile Creator's arms turned into dust.

"I thought you didn't have any powers?" Asked Cosmos.

"I guess... " said Creator. Her stabbed leg turned into dust. "I had it all along."

Whatever non-dusted part of Creator was there, dissolved completely into dust.

Cosmos looked at Miss Void and activated the green orb around his head. He rose up into the air and, though his hand didn't light up with energy, power seemed to radiate off him.

"That was the final straw Miss Void," Said Cosmos. "I won't spare you now."

Miss Void however, was not unfazed. She got up and her sword zoomed into her hand.

"Your friend is unconscious," she gestured to Brim, who was lying spread out on the space pod, "I trapped Indra and killed Creator. So the question is Cosmos, who's gonna kill me?"

"I am," he said.

Miss Void laughed. "Ha! You and what army? You certainly don't have the strength to fight me on your own."

Cosmos didn't respond. Instead, in the flash of a second, he created a green energy-fist that opened up its fingers. He sent it zooming towards Miss Void and grabbed her neck, then choked her.

"You see, I believe that actions speak louder than words. And if we're talking about an army, unlike you, I don't need one."

He let go off her, and she dropped to the ground. She held her neck and breathed heavily.

Then, Cosmos did what he did with the transportation beam, except instead of powering something up, he converted all that energy and molded it into a single destructive force.

He blasted it at Miss Void.

Maybe he had made it a bit too powerful, because half of the asteroid got blown up in one giant green explosion.

Even Cosmos had to look away.

After a few seconds, the debris cleared and Cosmos turned to look.

Along with half of the asteroid, Miss Void was gone too.

Chapter 24
The King of the Galaxy

It's very rare that movies, books or TV Shows show you what happened after the final battle.

Do you know why they do that?

Because it's pretty darn boring.

And that's why I won't either, because nothing very special happened.

I got you didn't I?

Of course something special happened, it's my story.

Cosmos healed Brim with his Celestial energy, and broke Indra's trap.

The Lord of the Sky then turned to face Cosmos. He had a stern expression on his face. But it wasn't an angry one.

"Cosmos," he said in a grand voice, "You have performed an extremely honorable feat by defeating the tyrant Miss Void, and thus restoring peace to the galaxy."

"Wasn't something like that said at the end of the original Star-Wars trilogy?"

"Shut up!" Said Indra. "Right where was I? Oh yeah, You have restored peace to the galaxy, and because you have performed this feat, you are now given the title of KING OF THE MILKY WAY!"

Cosmos stared at him. "What? No, shouldn't there be an election or something?"

"No, as long as you rule justly." Said the king of gods. "Besides, which hero tortures someone by making them count the votes of 50 Trillion beings?"

"Oh and one more thing," said Indra, "You are also given the title of 'Protector of the Multiverse!'"

"Wait, what? The Multiverse?"

"Oh yeah," said Indra. "Never heard of it?"

"No, I know what it is, but why am I supposed to protect it."

"You're the most capable Celestial in centuries. Don't argue, take the title."

"Okay, I, Cosmos, accept the title of 'Protector of the Multiverse.'"

"Oh and one more thing,"

"What?"

"You can't stay in this century anymore."

"What the heck do you mean?"

"I will have to send you back to the year twenty-twenty two. Don't worry, Miss Void won't be around. You'll still have your memories, but any of your current friends won't be alive. "

And so, Cosmos said his goodbyes to Brim and Indra, and then Indra pointed Vajra, his thunderbolt at him.

The last thing he saw was the back of his eyelids.

Chapter 25
It was all Just a Dream.
Or was it…?

Shawn Stephalla woke up with a start. He was drenched in sweat. He remembered his strange dream. How he saved the galaxy. The human mind was a strange and complex thing. How it formed an entire space odyssey just to tell Shawn how to deal with tragedies.

He decided that the dream was a sign. A sign that he should get back to living his normal life.

He got dressed and headed for work.

"Stephalla, nice to see you." Said the receptionist, Arthur.

"Nice to see you too, Arthur,"

While eating a bag of Cheetos from the vending machine, he got some powder on him. To wash it off, he headed for the washroom.

While washing his hands, he looked at his reflection and stepped back in shock.

He was the being from his dreams, the green skinned, armored, ball-headed being named Cosmos.

He looked down and saw that his hands were turning green. His entire body had turned green.

A metal plate formed on his chest that read 'Cosmos'.

His entire torso was covered in armor. A green sphere surrounded his head, and he turned into Cosmos.

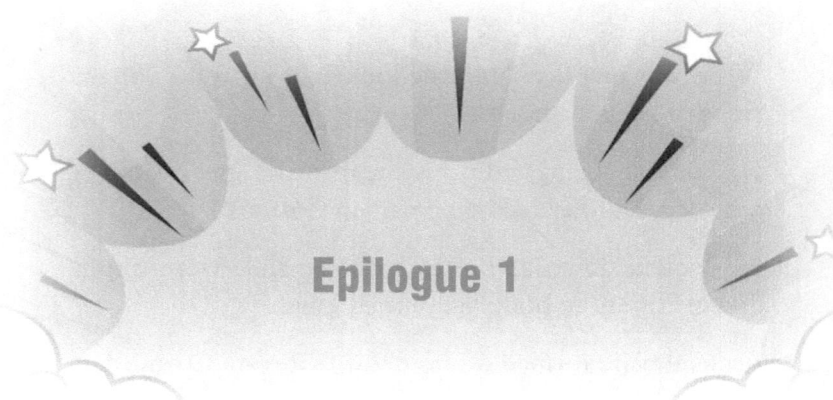

Epilogue 1

Brim stood in a meadow, which was basically an augmented pocket dimension, facing a block of stone. Tears welled up in his eyes seeing his great-great-great-great-great-great-great-great-great-grandfather's grave. Indra had made a pocket dimension for Snogglebrout's funeral at Brim's request.

Brim found that he had an annoying habit of letting his emotions lose at any random moment.

When Miss Void captured him, he should have been scared as heck, but he found himself enraged.

But now all his emotions seemed appropriate for the moment.

All his life, Brim had been told he was a disgrace to the word 'Neptunian.'

And after a while he had started to wonder if Snogglebrout would have believed that too. He wondered if his ancestor, who he idolized, would be ashamed of having a weak, short-heighted excuse of a descendant.

But he had learned to push that thought back.

But now, he realized he had never given himself a chance. Or rather, the Neptunians hadn't.

He'd been banned from the sword-righting club yet Bogglebrine still bullied him for not being good at sword fighting.

But he still managed to keep Miss Void at bay for enough time to let Indra rescue Cosmos.

And now, behind him stood the Galactic Army; before leaving, Cosmos had made Brim the chief of the army. The soldiers stood, with their heads bowed. Their new chief had told the soldiers to respect Snogglebrout for the hero he was.

But one of the best perks about this job was that now Bogglebrine had to treat Brim with the same respect he would give his boss.

Brim turned around and addressed the soldiers.

"Right," he said, "Our first plan of action is to go on each planet and tell them that this galaxy no longer has a ruler in this century. Cosmos will rule in his timeline, but he won't in this one."

"But sir, we need a ruler," said Bogglebrine.

"We don't. As long as we have an effective administrative system we won't. The army will still be around to protect the civilians from any threat that pops up. Did you understand Boggled-Brain?"

"My name's Bogglebrine!" The latter shouted.

Brim stared at him. If a weak looking dwarf stared down at you, you probably wouldn't take it seriously. However, Brim's stare would sell shivers down the spine of even a crab, and they didn't even have spine. "Did you just talk back to me?"

If Bogglebrine's looks could kill, then Brim would have been buried right here next to his ancestor. But then Bogglebrine bowed his head.

"No sir,"

Brim smiled.

Shawn pushed his glasses back to his eyes.

"Thank you so much doctor," said the woman.

"It's my pleasure Ms. Ortega. The symptoms you told me are definitely not linked to having a brain tumor, so there's absolutely no need to worry."

"I know it seems silly of me to even think that, but, you know, better safe than sorry!"

She chuckled. Shawn followed suit.

Whirrrrr!

A mechanical whirring sound seemed to come from Shawn. Oh no.

Lucia Ortega turned around in surprise. "What was that?"

Shawn looked furtively out of the window, as if to indicate that the noise was coming from there. He abruptly got up from his desk. He seemed hurried.

If he turned into his alter ego right here his secret would be revealed.

"I don't know. Would you excuse me, I need to go the washroo-

Shawn's eyes rolled up. He stopped in his tracks. Lucia Ortega's jaw dropped at what followed.

Shawn's skin began turning green, beige armor formed at his torso, a red cape wrapped itself around his neck.

A green dome formed around his head.

Cosmos stretched his arms and took a deep breath.

"What the heck!" Screamed the woman. "What's happening Doctor...

She read the new metal nameplate on his chest that read:

Cosmos

"... Cosmos?"

The being smiled. "Doctor... Cosmos. Doctor Cosmos." He laughed. "I like that name."

Suddenly, a sign flashed before his eyes that read:

Alert Message from Amravati! Lord Indra Needs Help!

Dr. Cosmos summoned his signature green beam.

The green beam flashed down upon him and retracted back, leaving Lucia Ortega all alone in Shawn Stephalla's clinic.

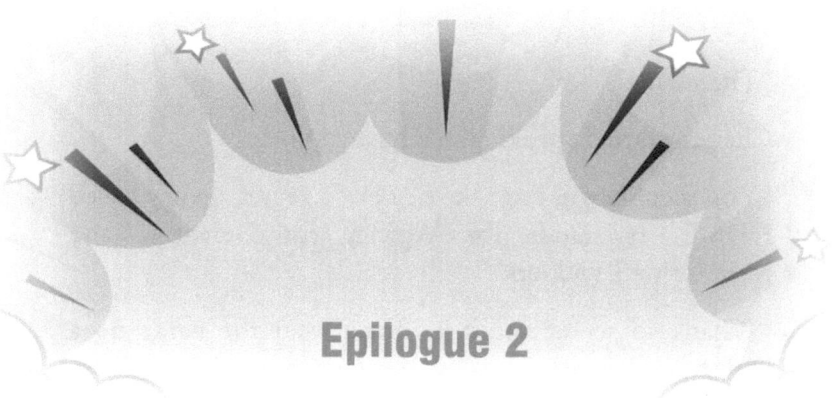

Epilogue 2

The nurse told him that a man wanted to meet Shawn. She told him that the man was waiting in his clinic.

Once Shawn walked into the clinic, he saw a man sitting on a chair in front of the desk.

The man seemed to be in his late forties. He had brown hair and a brown beard.

He wore a three-piece suit, with black trousers and sleek brown shoes. There was a badge on his suit that said 'ADME'.

The man got up and extended his hand. Shawn shook it.

"Allow me to introduce myself, my name is Michael Cherian."

"Good afternoon, Mr. Cherian, so tell me what problem you are having."

"Oh, I'm not here for medical reasons."

"Then what?"

Cherian started speaking in a hushed voice.

"You see, Shawn, I am the head of a secret agency called ADME. It stands for 'Agency for Defeating and Monitoring Evildoers'."

"What's so secret about it if you wear the name on a badge?"

"Oh, I tell everyone that it's the name of a company called, 'Aviation Department of the Manhattan Environment'. So, the reason I wanted to talk to you is this-

My agency has noticed that you sometimes turn into a green bodied super-hero. I disregarded their words thinking that superheroes don't exist. But then your friend Powerbolt came to my attention. And his alien friend Optico. However, I still had my doubts. Hence, I sent my agent Lucia Ortega to meet you firsthand, and was surprised when she reported that she saw you turn into a 'Celestial'."

Shawn swallowed. "So, what do you want from me?"

"I am assembling a strike team, and I'm looking for beings who have some sort of power that is above the strength of normal humans."

"So, we're like the dollar-store avengers?"

"You can think of it like that. Though I must say, being called the dollar-store Nick Fury is a source of immense pride. So, the question is Dr. Stephalla, do you want to join?"

"What's the name of the team?"

"It's called the Super-Squad."

"Hmm. But why?"

"The world has many problems Mr. Stephalla. I'm sure everyone agrees with that. The only 'peace' we have is superficial and can be shattered by a quarrel between two leaders. Imagine someday the Earth faces an external threat. With everybody at each other's throats, how will we save ourselves? We need a higher, superior team of beings. Beings that cannot be defeated with something as simple as a well-aimed bullet."

"Your points seem valid. Where do I sign?"

"Awesome! I will share the paperwork shortly!"

Micheal Cherian got up, shook hands with Shawn and proceeded to leave the room.

"Mr. Cherian, can we discuss this further, maybe over a cup of coffee?"

He smirked. "I would love to Shawn, but I'm already late. I have an appointment with your friend Powerbolt after this!"

Glossary

Banbrine- A Neptunian soldier in the Galactic Army that has a feud with Snogglebrout. He is also reported to be extremely annoying and a pain in neck.

Bogglebrine- A descendant of Banbrine. If you took all the bad qualities of the former, removed the little good qualities there were and added a little extra chubbiness you would get Bogglebrine. His personal hobbies include drinking sugary beverages, sword fighting and bullying Brim.

Celestial Tangle-When two Celestials unleash their maximum power and direct a destructive blast of energy at each other, their walls of energy get tangled up and constantly try to overpower the other. If any Celestial's power weakens, they could be sent flying all the way to a different multiverse.

Council of Ministers- A group of ministers that advise the king of the galaxy.

Galactic Jail- A massive prison the size of Asia located on the planet Pluto. Its walls are impenetrable, and any sort of energy, magic or power fails to blast through it.

Galactic Palace- A palace located deep within the heart of the sun, which houses the king, his servants, the Council of Ministers, the royal court, and any guests the king wishes to host.

Lord Indra- Indra, a key deity in Hinduism, governs rain, storms, thunder, lightning, and war. As the king of the gods and ruler of Svarga (heaven), he wields a thunderbolt (Vajra) and possesses symbols like a discus, axe, and elephant goad. In the ancient Vedic tradition, Indra holds a prominent role, presiding over the celestial realm from the city of Amaravati.

Neptunian- A species of beings from the planet Neptune.

Royal Court- A collective assembly which comprises of the Council of Ministers, the Main Minister, the king of the galaxy, And a few important generals from the army.

Shrui- Lord Indra's fortune teller. Like the typical fortune teller, her prophecies come out in the form of poems that would make William Shakespear blush.

Space Pod- The vehicle which the soldiers of the Galactic Army use to commute. Some special space pods are loaded with inbuilt weapons or can travel at extreme speeds.

Space Ray Blaster- A weapon used by the soldiers of the Galactic Army that fires laser beams.

Time Dilation- Time dilation is a phenomenon in which time passes at different rates depending on the speed and gravity of an object. According to Einstein's theory of relativity, time moves slower for objects in motion or under strong gravitational forces. This means that time can appear to pass more slowly for someone in a fast-moving spaceship or near a massive celestial body.

Toirstarin- A not so small town on the planet Neptune.

Uchchaishravas- Uchchaishravas emerged during the churning of the ocean (Samudra Manthan) by the gods (devas) and demons (asuras). This divine horse is often described as a seven-headed, pure white horse and is considered extremely rare and auspicious. Uchchaishravas eventually became the mount (vahana) of Lord Indra, the king of the gods. The horse is associated with prosperity and is considered a symbol of wealth in Hindu mythology. Uchchaishravas is sometimes portrayed in various Hindu epics and stories, contributing to the rich tapestry of mythical creatures within the tradition.

However, leaving divinity aside, each seven head of this equine creature is infamous for its snarky sarcastic comments.

WANT TO GET A PROPER INTRODUCTION TO LORD INDRA AND SEE MORE OF SHRUI AND UCHCHAISHRAVAS?

WANT TO KNOW WHAT HAPPENED IN AMRAVATI?

CHECK OUT POWER-BOLT, MY FIRST BOOK!

IT'S ALREADY AVAILABLE ON AMAZON, KINDLE, GOOGLE BOOKS AND GOOGLE PLAY!

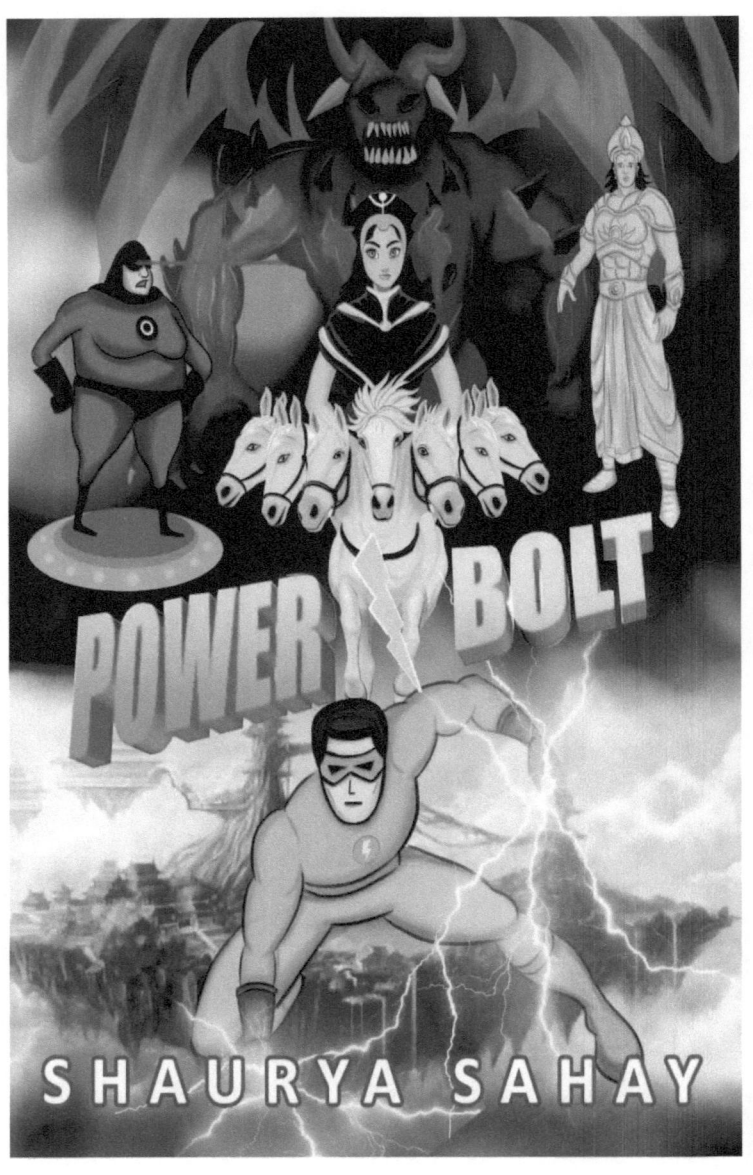

About the Author

An avid reader himself, Shaurya Sahay got his first book published when he was 10 years old. He has spent the majority of his formative years immersed in books, making animations, and playing music on the keyboard. His passion for the superhero-fantasy genre is evident, fueled by his ardent love for all things Marvel.

He is a Potterhead and now has also finished reading the Riordanverse by Rick Riordan, the Aru Shah series by Roshini Chokshi, and Amish Tripathi's Shiva Trilogy and Ram Chandra series.

He has an innate gift to imagine the start and end of the story and then pen it down, chapter by chapter, holding the threads together to present a wonderful fiction for his readers that he has lovingly created through his stories.

In this book, Shaurya extends an invitation to readers to step into his realm, where stories and characters come to life. As he shares his world with you, he eagerly anticipates welcoming more readers into the universe he has crafted.

Welcome to the fantasy world where mythology meets fiction and we seamlessly travel from Earth to another realm, one beyond the limits of imagination.

www.ingramcontent.com/pod-product-compliance
Lightning Source LLC
LaVergne TN
LVHW041608070526
838199LV00052B/3039